P9-CAL-733

SUMMER CAMP
SCIENCE
MYSTERIES

#1 **In Search**
of the **Fog Zombie**

A Mystery about Matter

by Lynda Beauregard

illustrated by Der-shing Helmer

GRAPHIC UNIVERSE™ • MINNEAPOLIS • NEW YORK

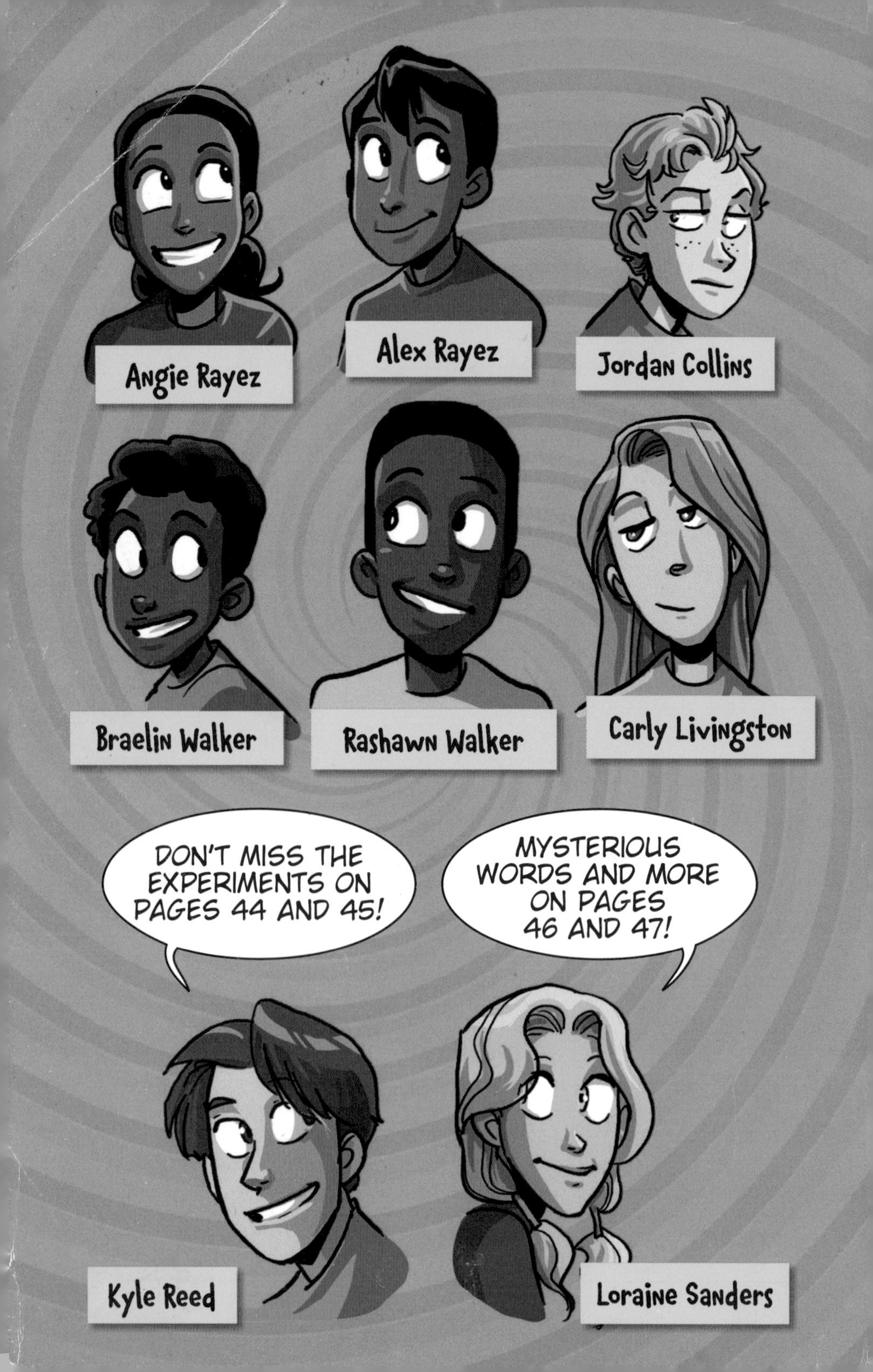
Angie Rayez
Alex Rayez
Jordan Collins
Braelin Walker
Rashawn Walker
Carly Livingston
DON'T MISS THE EXPERIMENTS ON PAGES 44 AND 45!
MYSTERIOUS WORDS AND MORE ON PAGES 46 AND 47!
Kyle Reed
Loraine Sanders

Matter is the stuff that everything is made from. It can take the form of a solid, liquid, or gas. Some matter, such as water, can change back and forth between these three states if it gets hotter or colder.

All matter takes up space and has mass. (Mass is what gives things weight, together with the force of gravity, which pulls objects toward Earth's surface.) Matter is made up of atoms. There are more than 100 different kinds of atoms, or elements. They each have different properties and names. Atoms can also join together to form molecules.

Story by Lynda Beauregard
Art by Der-shing Helmer
Coloring by Jenn Manley Lee
Lettering by Grace Lu

Copyright © 2012 by Lerner Publishing Group, Inc.

Graphic Universe™ is a trademark of Lerner Publishing Group, Inc.

All rights reserved. International copyright secured. No part of this book may be reproduced, stored in a retrieval system, or transmitted in any form or by any means—electronic, mechanical, photocopying, recording, or otherwise—without the prior written permission of Lerner Publishing Group, Inc., except for the inclusion of brief quotations in an acknowledged review.

Graphic Universe™
A division of Lerner Publishing Group, Inc.
241 First Avenue North
Minneapolis, MN 55401 U.S.A.

Website address: www.lernerbooks.com

Main body text set in CCWildwords.
Typeface provided by Comicraft/Active Images.

Library of Congress Cataloging-in-Publication Data

Beauregard, Lynda.
    In search of the Fog Zombie : a mystery about matter / by Lynda Beauregard ; illustrated by Der-shing Helmer.
        p.   cm. — (Summer camp science mysteries, #1)
        Summary: When Angie and Alex arrive at Camp Dakota, a thick fog envelops everything and when the campers start finding mysterious notes with hints about a Fog Zombie, their counselors teach them about solids, liquids, gases, and the properties of matter to uncover the meaning of the clues. Includes glossary and experiments.
        ISBN: 978–0–7613–5689–9 (lib. bdg. : alk. paper)
        1. Graphic novels. [1. Graphic novels. 2. Camps—Fiction. 3. Matter—Fiction.] I. Helmer, Der-shing, ill. II. Title.
    PZ7.7.B42In 2012
    741.5'973—dc23   2011022374

Manufactured in the United States of America
1 – CG – 12/31/11

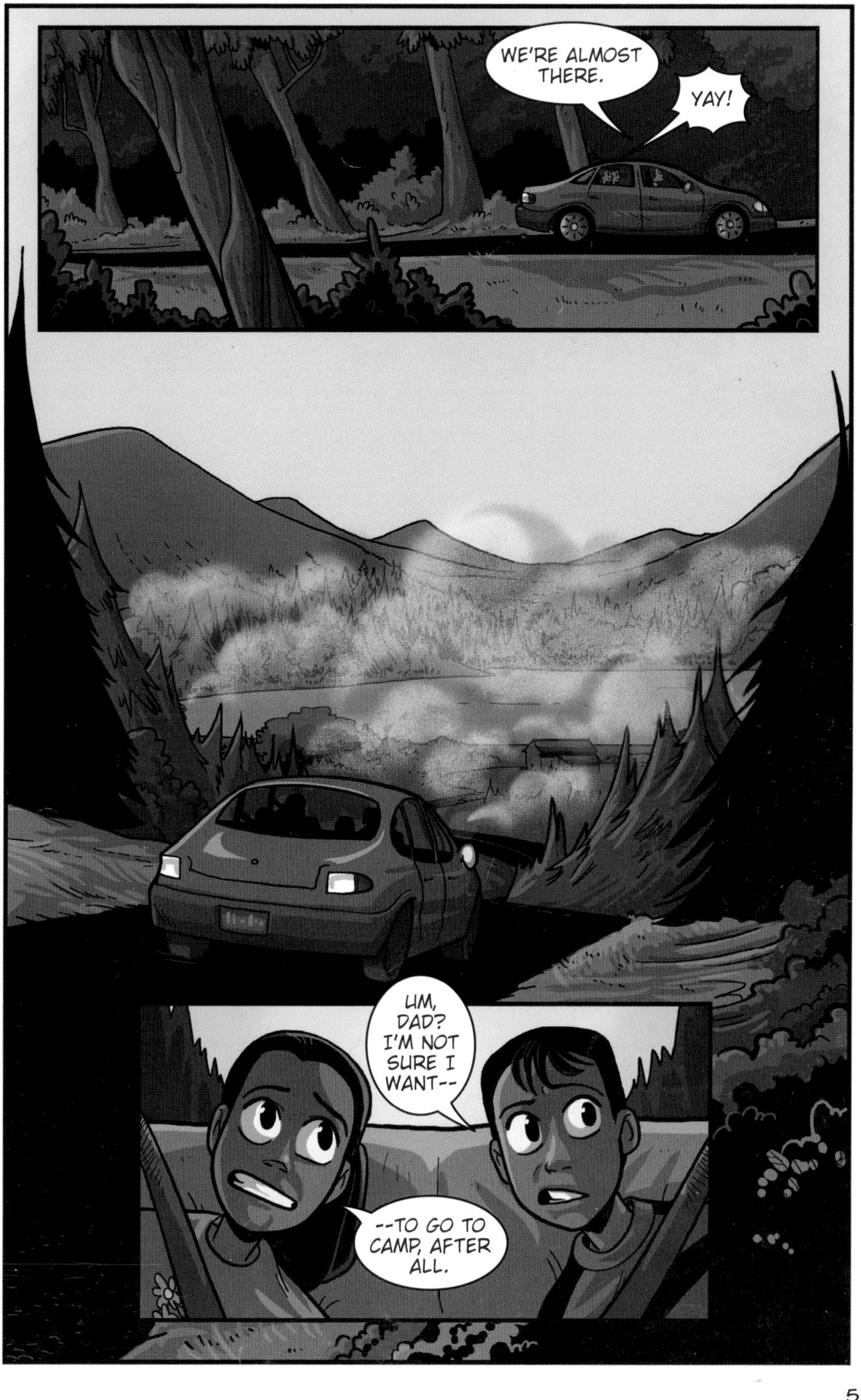
WE'RE ALMOST THERE.
YAY!
UM, DAD? I'M NOT SURE I WANT--
--TO GO TO CAMP, AFTER ALL.

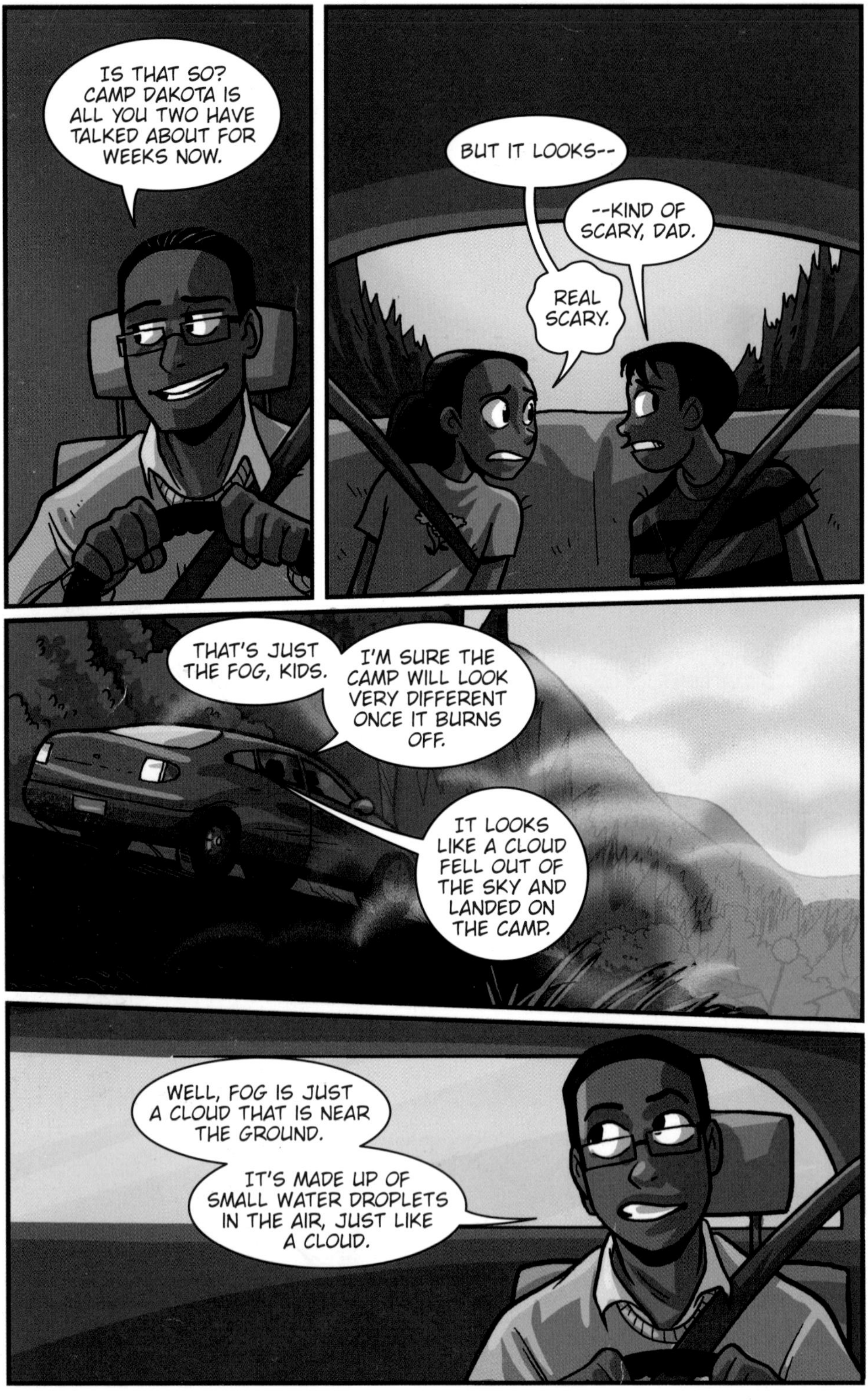
IS THAT SO? CAMP DAKOTA IS ALL YOU TWO HAVE TALKED ABOUT FOR WEEKS NOW.
BUT IT LOOKS--
--KIND OF SCARY, DAD.
REAL SCARY.
THAT'S JUST THE FOG, KIDS.
I'M SURE THE CAMP WILL LOOK VERY DIFFERENT ONCE IT BURNS OFF.
IT LOOKS LIKE A CLOUD FELL OUT OF THE SKY AND LANDED ON THE CAMP.
WELL, FOG IS JUST A CLOUD THAT IS NEAR THE GROUND.
IT'S MADE UP OF SMALL WATER DROPLETS IN THE AIR, JUST LIKE A CLOUD.

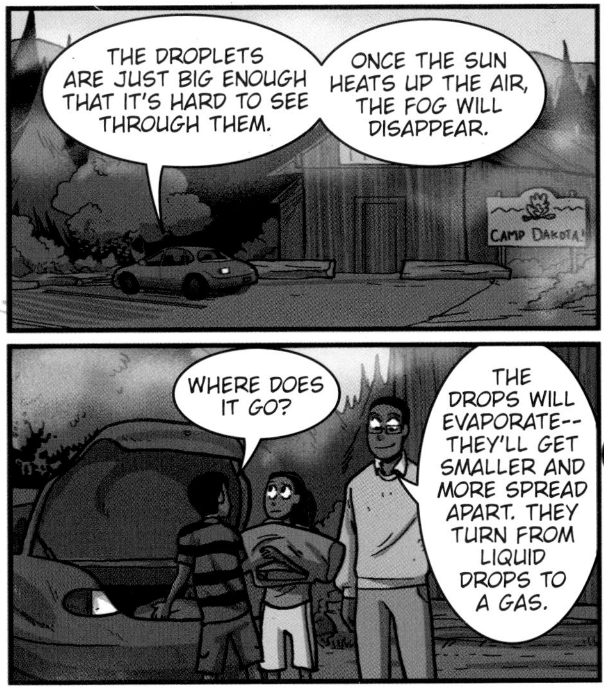
THE DROPLETS ARE JUST BIG ENOUGH THAT IT'S HARD TO SEE THROUGH THEM.
ONCE THE SUN HEATS UP THE AIR, THE FOG WILL DISAPPEAR.
CAMP DAKOTA!
WHERE DOES IT GO?
THE DROPS WILL EVAPORATE--THEY'LL GET SMALLER AND MORE SPREAD APART. THEY TURN FROM LIQUID DROPS TO A GAS.

Evaporation occurs when warmer temperatures cause water to change from a liquid to a gas. This gas is called water vapor. Cooler air makes the vapor molecules clump together and turn back into water drops. This change from gas to liquid is called condensation.

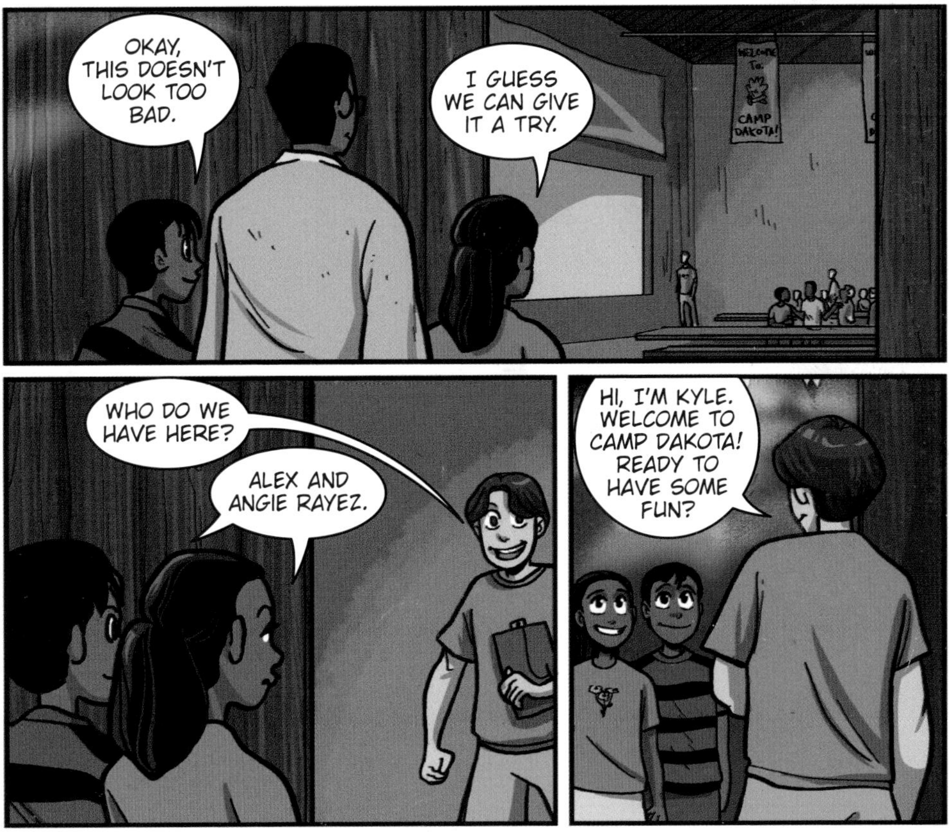
OKAY, THIS DOESN'T LOOK TOO BAD.
I GUESS WE CAN GIVE IT A TRY.
CAMP DAKOTA!
WHO DO WE HAVE HERE?
ALEX AND ANGIE RAYEZ.
HI, I'M KYLE. WELCOME TO CAMP DAKOTA! READY TO HAVE SOME FUN?

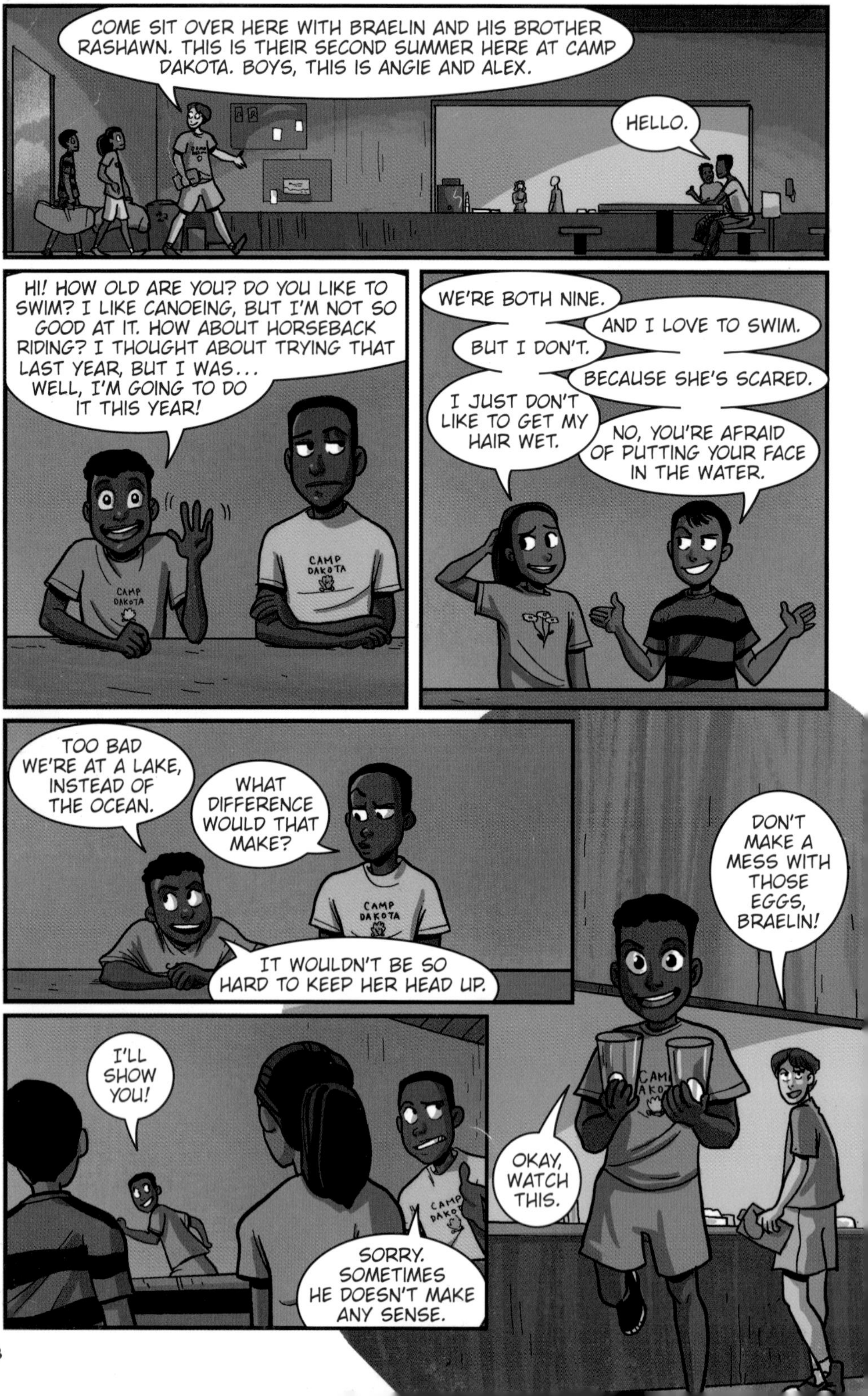
COME SIT OVER HERE WITH BRAELIN AND HIS BROTHER RASHAWN. THIS IS THEIR SECOND SUMMER HERE AT CAMP DAKOTA. BOYS, THIS IS ANGIE AND ALEX.
HELLO.
HI! HOW OLD ARE YOU? DO YOU LIKE TO SWIM? I LIKE CANOEING, BUT I'M NOT SO GOOD AT IT. HOW ABOUT HORSEBACK RIDING? I THOUGHT ABOUT TRYING THAT LAST YEAR, BUT I WAS... WELL, I'M GOING TO DO IT THIS YEAR!
CAMP DAKOTA
CAMP DAKOTA
WE'RE BOTH NINE.
AND I LOVE TO SWIM.
BUT I DON'T.
BECAUSE SHE'S SCARED.
I JUST DON'T LIKE TO GET MY HAIR WET.
NO, YOU'RE AFRAID OF PUTTING YOUR FACE IN THE WATER.
TOO BAD WE'RE AT A LAKE, INSTEAD OF THE OCEAN.
WHAT DIFFERENCE WOULD THAT MAKE?
CAMP DAKOTA
IT WOULDN'T BE SO HARD TO KEEP HER HEAD UP.
DON'T MAKE A MESS WITH THOSE EGGS, BRAELIN!
I'LL SHOW YOU!
OKAY, WATCH THIS.
SORRY. SOMETIMES HE DOESN'T MAKE ANY SENSE.

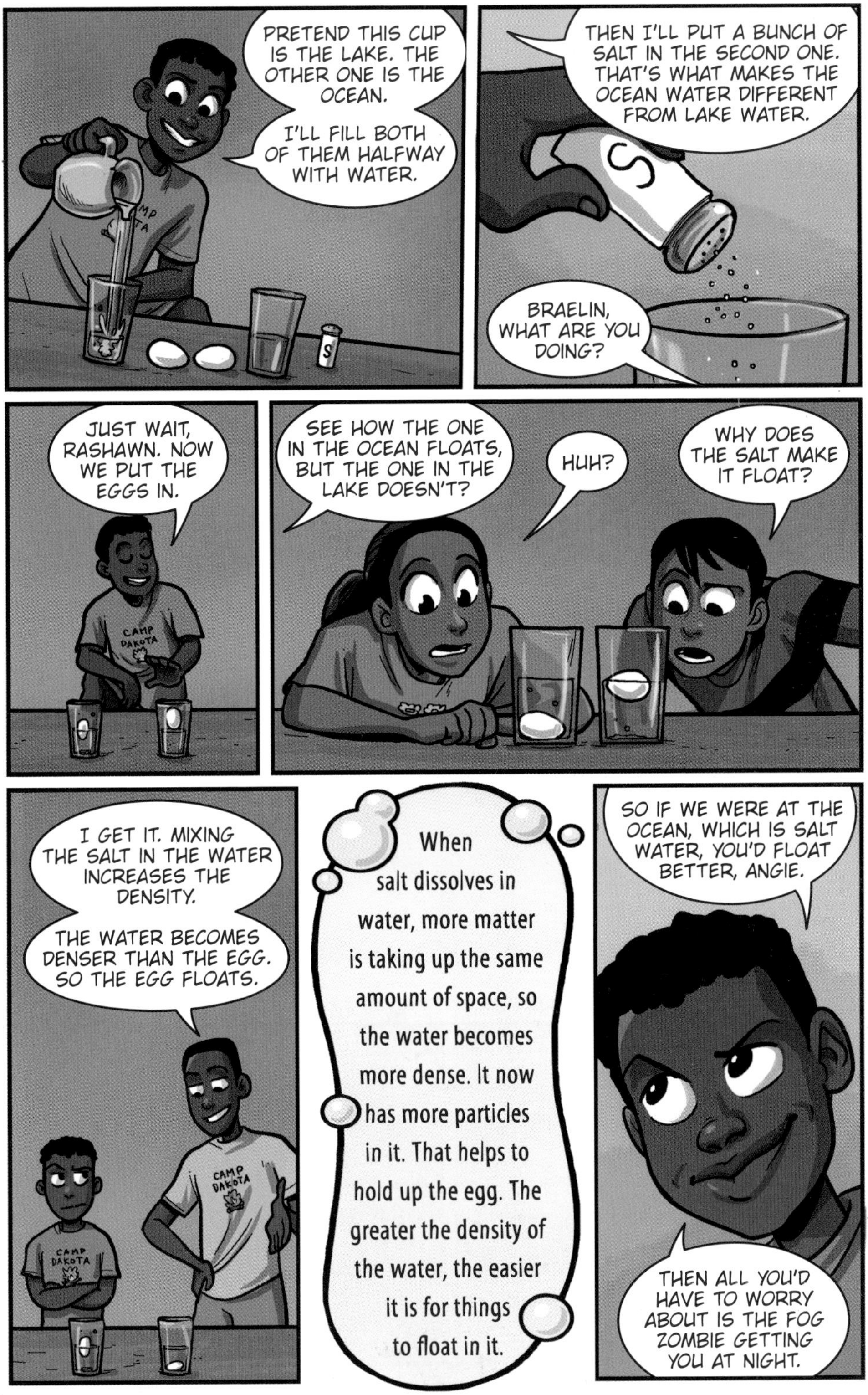

PRETEND THIS CUP IS THE LAKE. THE OTHER ONE IS THE OCEAN.
I'LL FILL BOTH OF THEM HALFWAY WITH WATER.
THEN I'LL PUT A BUNCH OF SALT IN THE SECOND ONE. THAT'S WHAT MAKES THE OCEAN WATER DIFFERENT FROM LAKE WATER.
BRAELIN, WHAT ARE YOU DOING?
JUST WAIT, RASHAWN. NOW WE PUT THE EGGS IN.
SEE HOW THE ONE IN THE OCEAN FLOATS, BUT THE ONE IN THE LAKE DOESN'T?
HUH?
WHY DOES THE SALT MAKE IT FLOAT?
I GET IT. MIXING THE SALT IN THE WATER INCREASES THE DENSITY.
THE WATER BECOMES DENSER THAN THE EGG. SO THE EGG FLOATS.
When salt dissolves in water, more matter is taking up the same amount of space, so the water becomes more dense. It now has more particles in it. That helps to hold up the egg. The greater the density of the water, the easier it is for things to float in it.
SO IF WE WERE AT THE OCEAN, WHICH IS SALT WATER, YOU'D FLOAT BETTER, ANGIE.
THEN ALL YOU'D HAVE TO WORRY ABOUT IS THE FOG ZOMBIE GETTING YOU AT NIGHT.

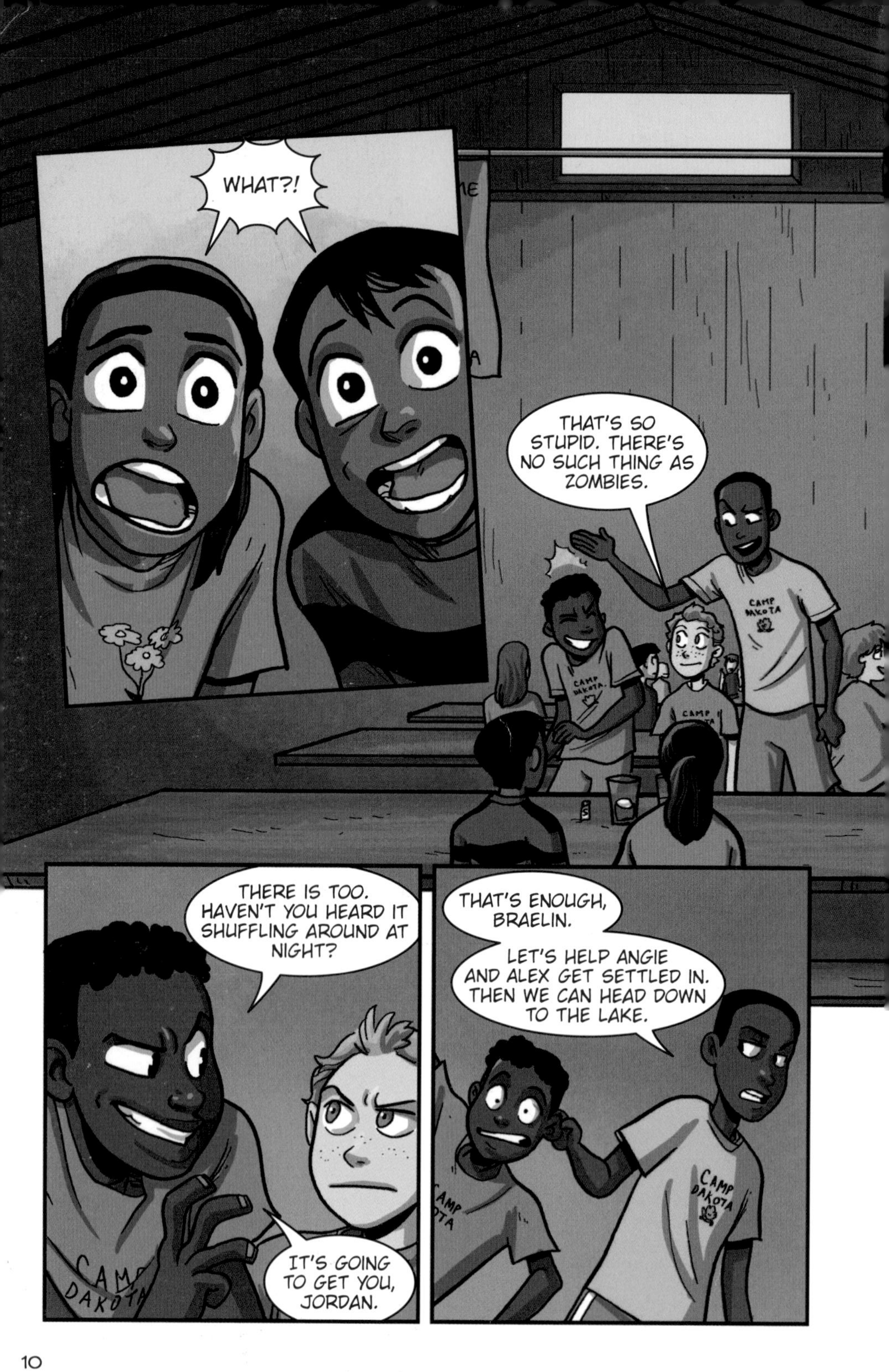
WHAT?!
THAT'S SO STUPID. THERE'S NO SUCH THING AS ZOMBIES.
THERE IS TOO. HAVEN'T YOU HEARD IT SHUFFLING AROUND AT NIGHT?
IT'S GOING TO GET YOU, JORDAN.
THAT'S ENOUGH, BRAELIN.
LET'S HELP ANGIE AND ALEX GET SETTLED IN. THEN WE CAN HEAD DOWN TO THE LAKE.

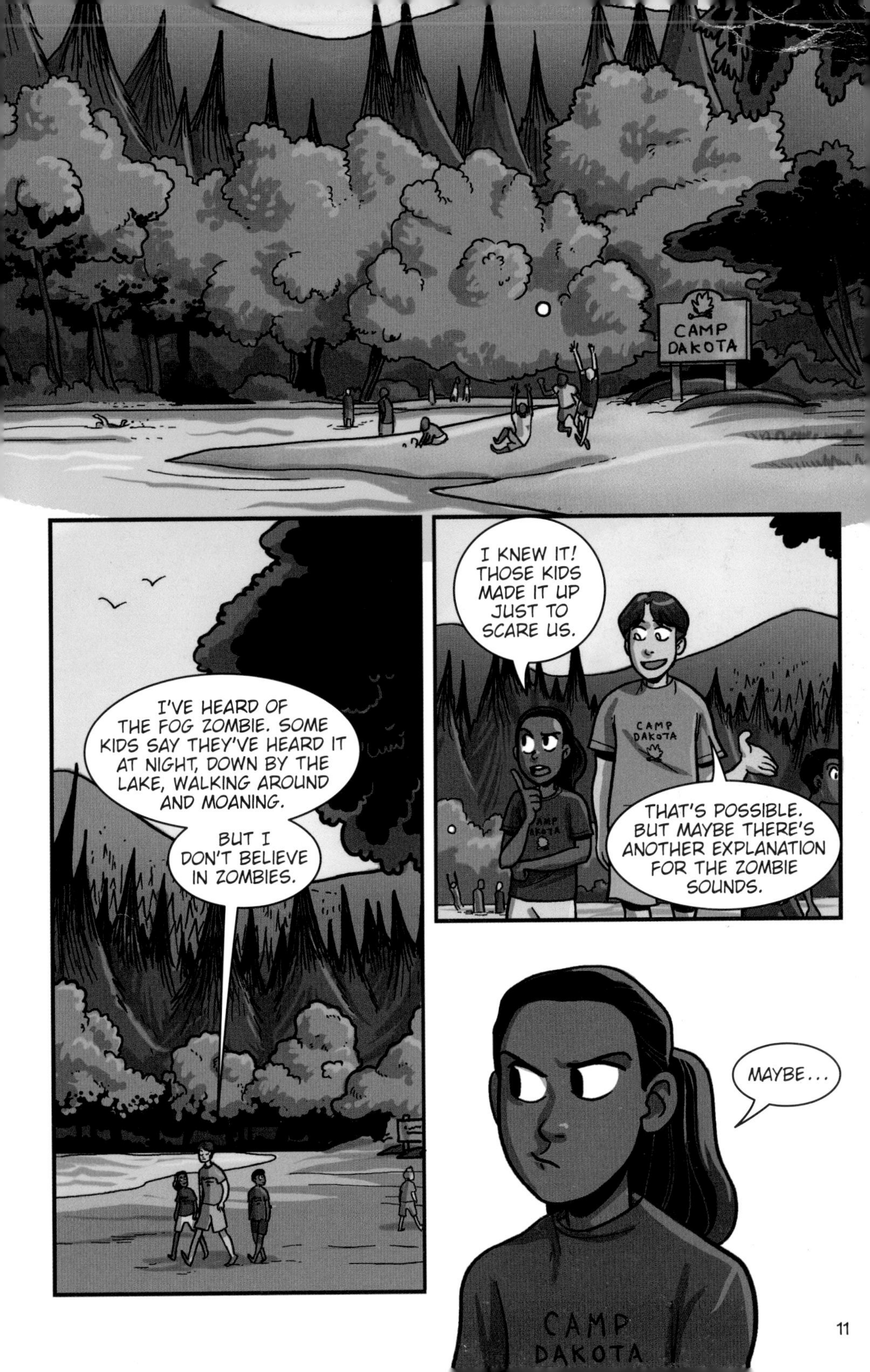
CAMP DAKOTA
I'VE HEARD OF THE FOG ZOMBIE. SOME KIDS SAY THEY'VE HEARD IT AT NIGHT, DOWN BY THE LAKE, WALKING AROUND AND MOANING.
BUT I DON'T BELIEVE IN ZOMBIES.
I KNEW IT! THOSE KIDS MADE IT UP JUST TO SCARE US.
CAMP DAKOTA
THAT'S POSSIBLE. BUT MAYBE THERE'S ANOTHER EXPLANATION FOR THE ZOMBIE SOUNDS.
MAYBE...
CAMP DAKOTA

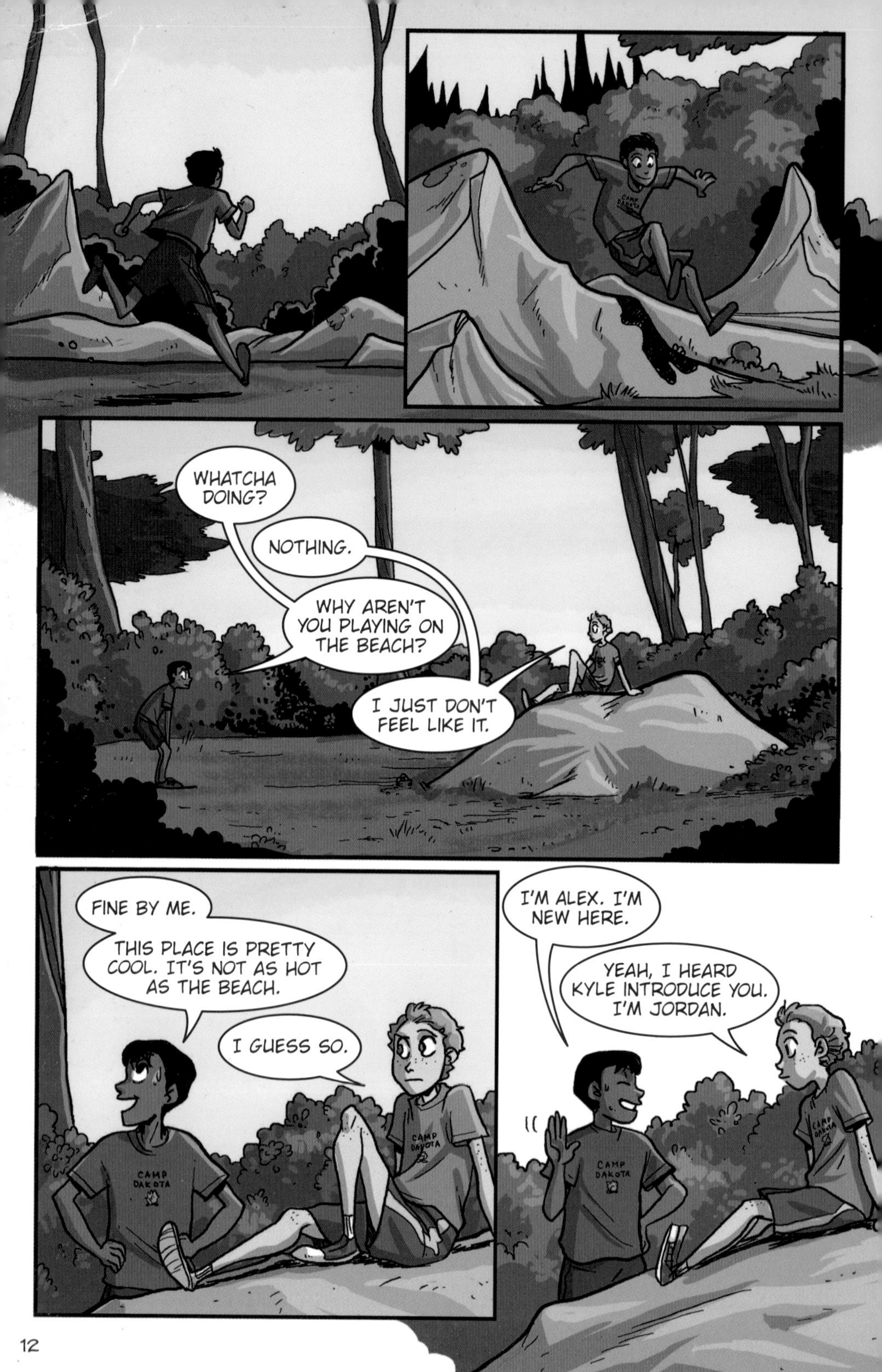
WHATCHA DOING?
NOTHING.
WHY AREN'T YOU PLAYING ON THE BEACH?
I JUST DON'T FEEL LIKE IT.
FINE BY ME.
THIS PLACE IS PRETTY COOL. IT'S NOT AS HOT AS THE BEACH.
I GUESS SO.
I'M ALEX. I'M NEW HERE.
YEAH, I HEARD KYLE INTRODUCE YOU. I'M JORDAN.

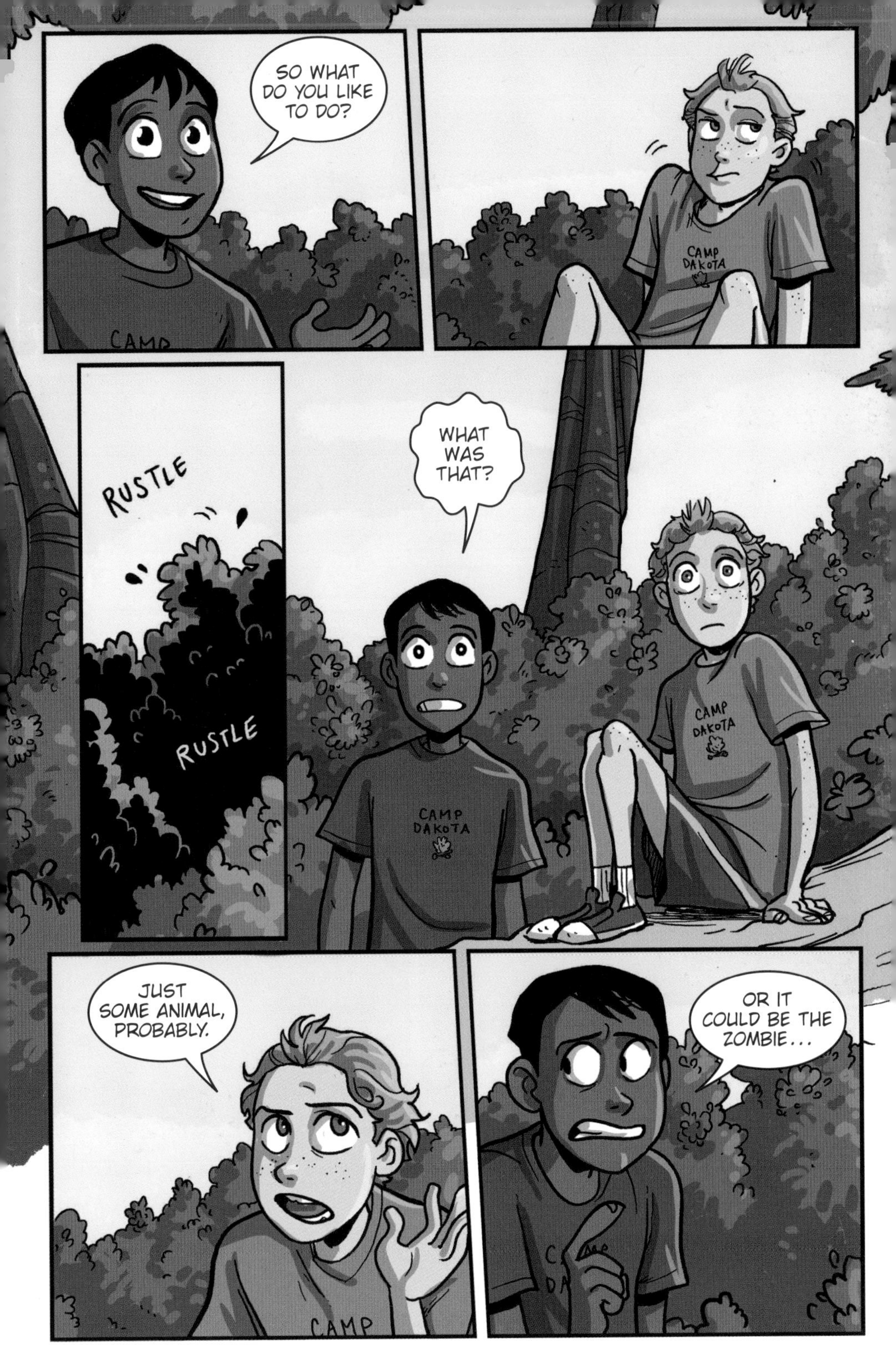
SO WHAT DO YOU LIKE TO DO?
RUSTLE
RUSTLE
WHAT WAS THAT?
JUST SOME ANIMAL, PROBABLY.
OR IT COULD BE THE ZOMBIE...

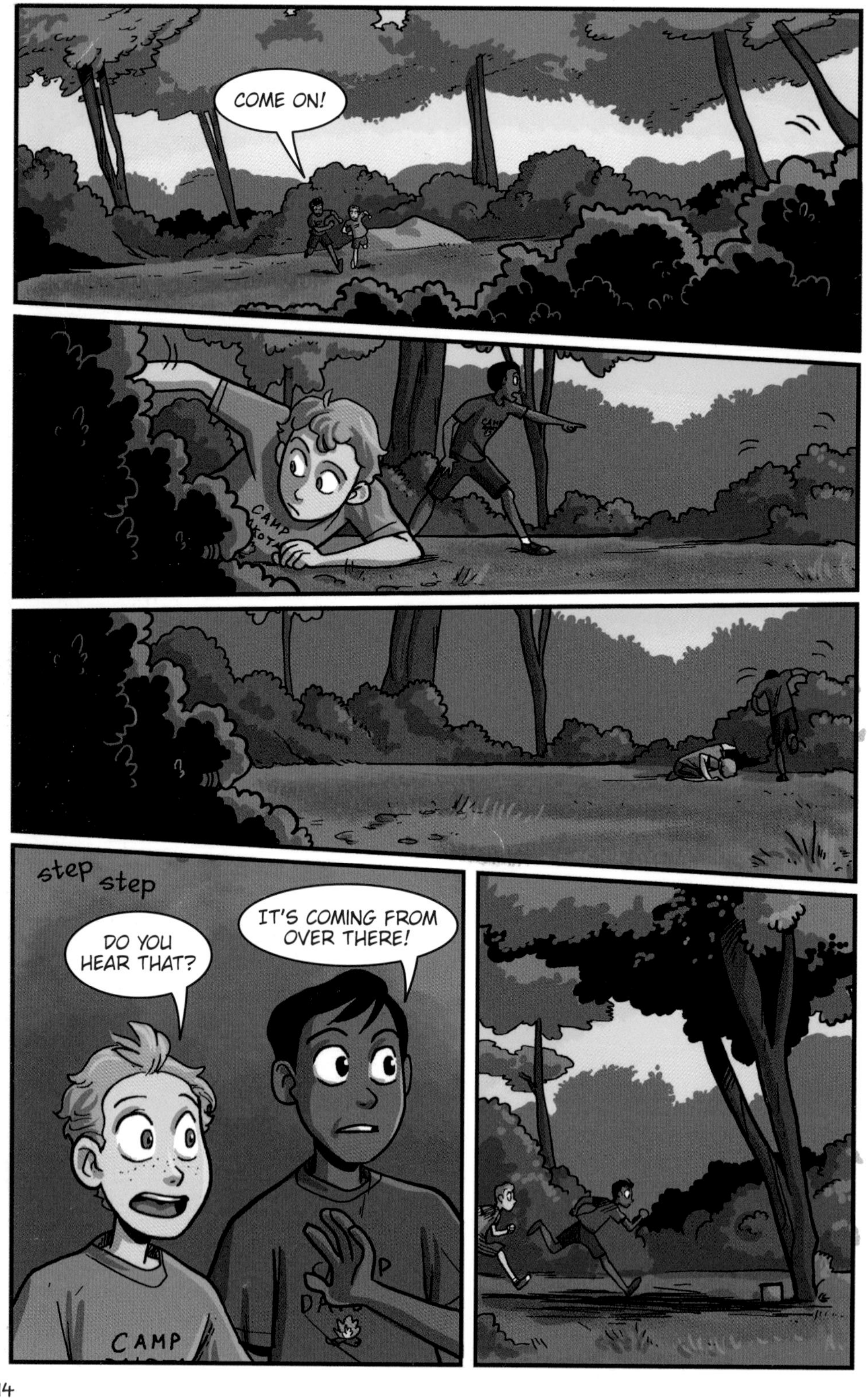
COME ON!
step step
DO YOU HEAR THAT?
IT'S COMING FROM OVER THERE!

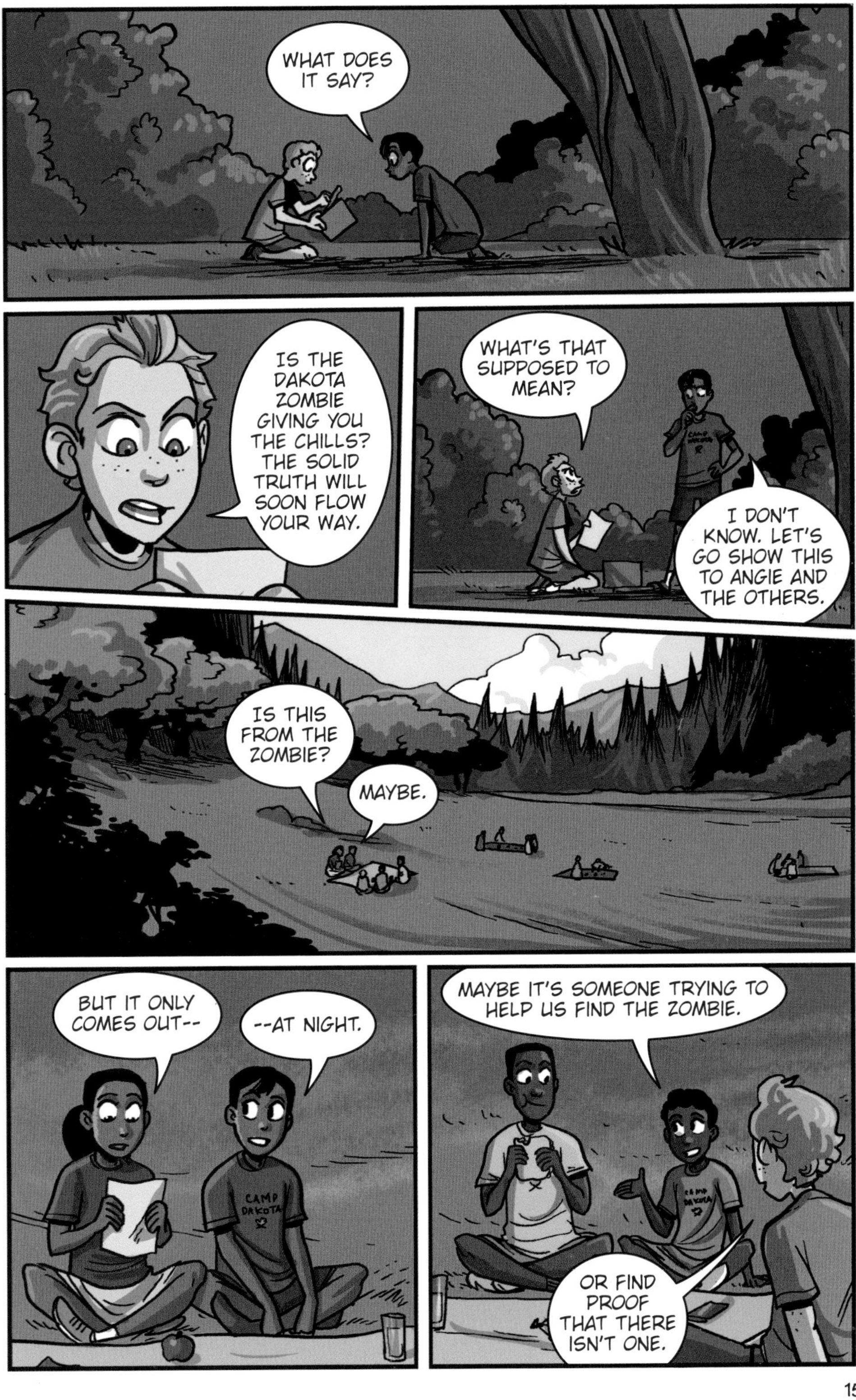
WHAT DOES IT SAY?
IS THE DAKOTA ZOMBIE GIVING YOU THE CHILLS? THE SOLID TRUTH WILL SOON FLOW YOUR WAY.
WHAT'S THAT SUPPOSED TO MEAN?
I DON'T KNOW. LET'S GO SHOW THIS TO ANGIE AND THE OTHERS.
IS THIS FROM THE ZOMBIE?
MAYBE.
BUT IT ONLY COMES OUT--
--AT NIGHT.
CAMP DAKOTA
MAYBE IT'S SOMEONE TRYING TO HELP US FIND THE ZOMBIE.
OR FIND PROOF THAT THERE ISN'T ONE.

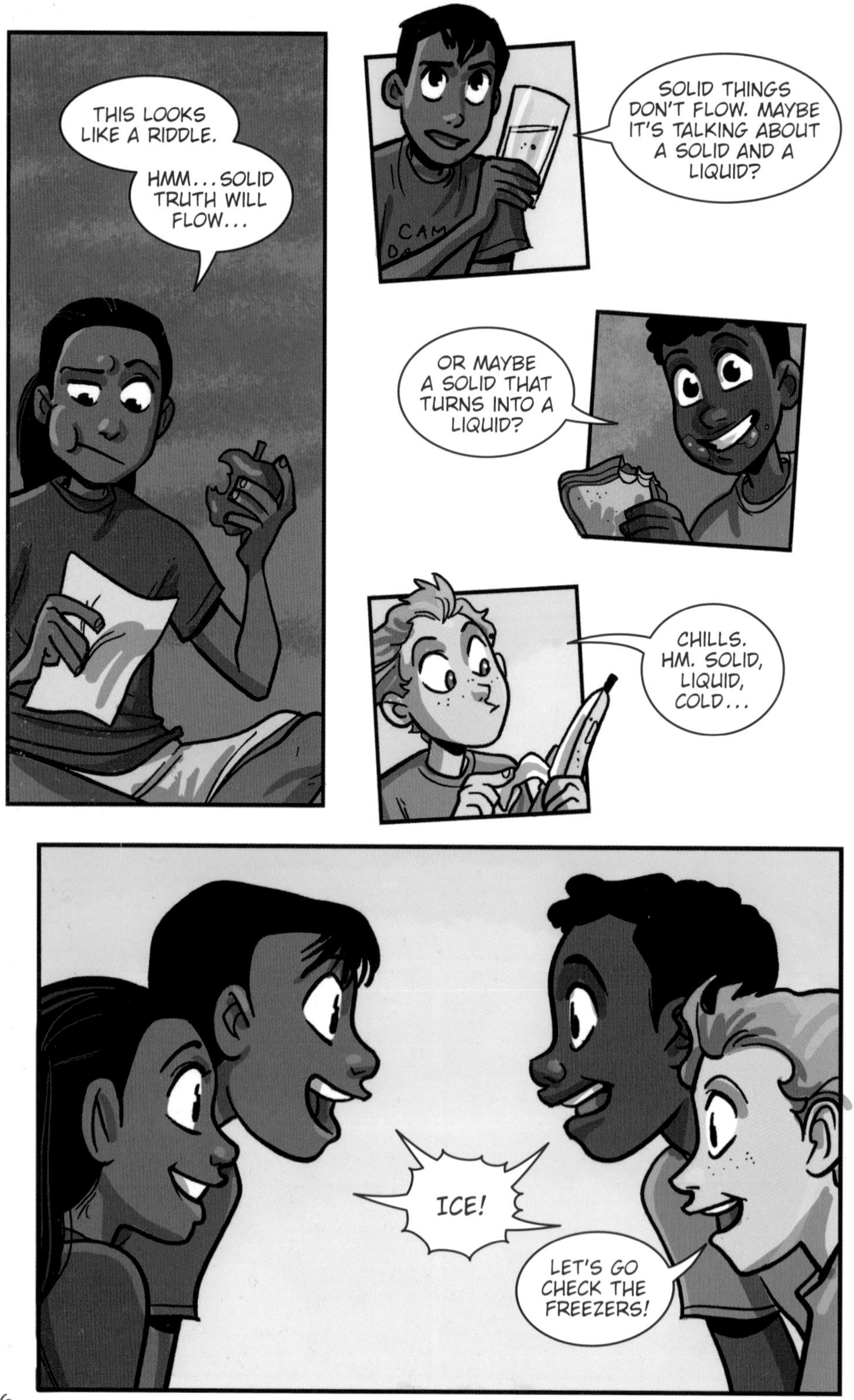
THIS LOOKS LIKE A RIDDLE.
HMM... SOLID TRUTH WILL FLOW...
SOLID THINGS DON'T FLOW. MAYBE IT'S TALKING ABOUT A SOLID AND A LIQUID?
OR MAYBE A SOLID THAT TURNS INTO A LIQUID?
CHILLS. HM. SOLID, LIQUID, COLD...
ICE!
LET'S GO CHECK THE FREEZERS!

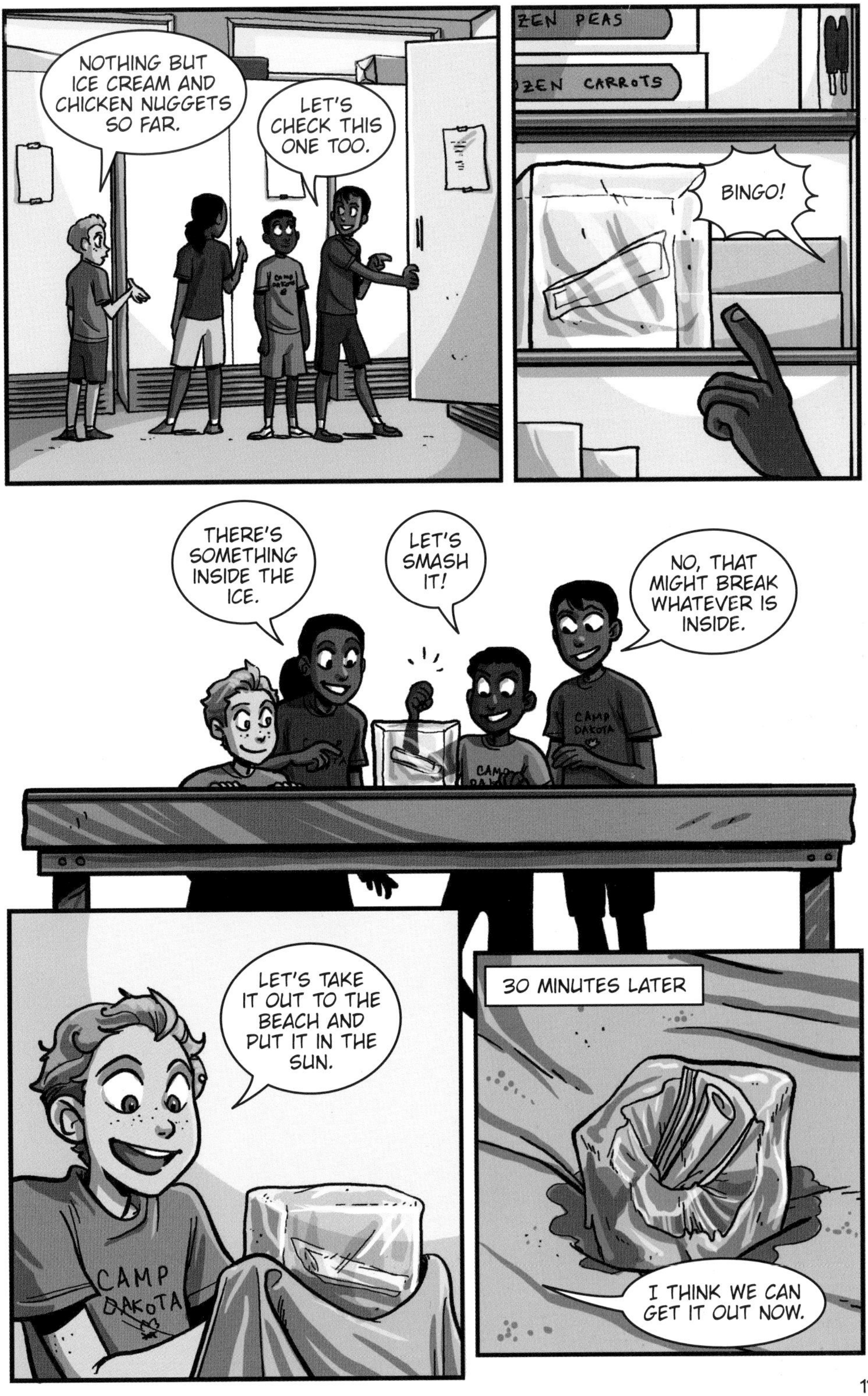
NOTHING BUT ICE CREAM AND CHICKEN NUGGETS SO FAR.
LET'S CHECK THIS ONE TOO.
ZEN PEAS
ZEN CARROTS
BINGO!
THERE'S SOMETHING INSIDE THE ICE.
LET'S SMASH IT!
NO, THAT MIGHT BREAK WHATEVER IS INSIDE.
CAMP DAKOTA
LET'S TAKE IT OUT TO THE BEACH AND PUT IT IN THE SUN.
CAMP DAKOTA
30 MINUTES LATER
I THINK WE CAN GET IT OUT NOW.

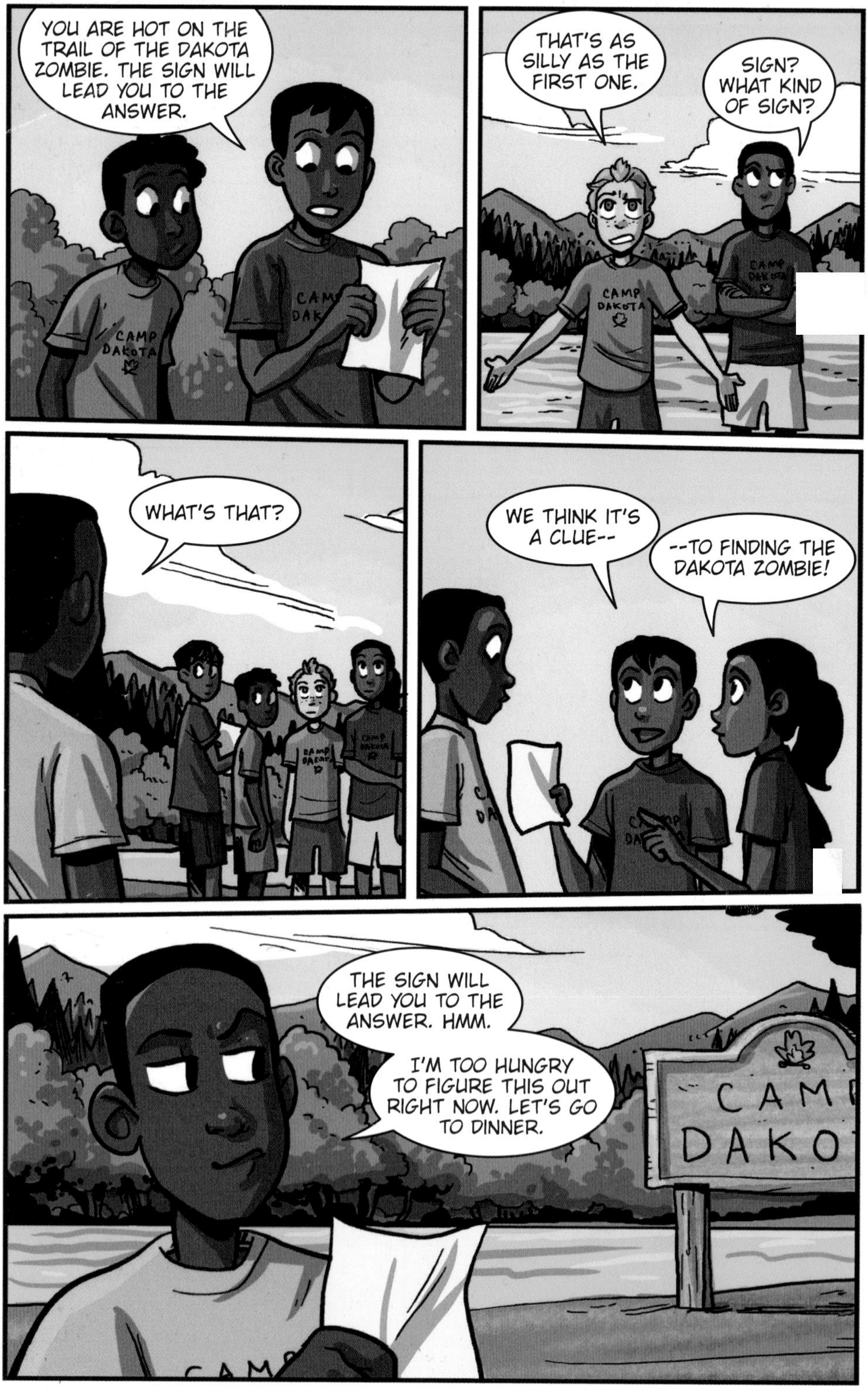
YOU ARE HOT ON THE TRAIL OF THE DAKOTA ZOMBIE. THE SIGN WILL LEAD YOU TO THE ANSWER.
CAMP DAKOTA
THAT'S AS SILLY AS THE FIRST ONE.
SIGN? WHAT KIND OF SIGN?
CAMP DAKOTA
WHAT'S THAT?
WE THINK IT'S A CLUE--
--TO FINDING THE DAKOTA ZOMBIE!
THE SIGN WILL LEAD YOU TO THE ANSWER. HMM.
I'M TOO HUNGRY TO FIGURE THIS OUT RIGHT NOW. LET'S GO TO DINNER.
CAM
DAKO

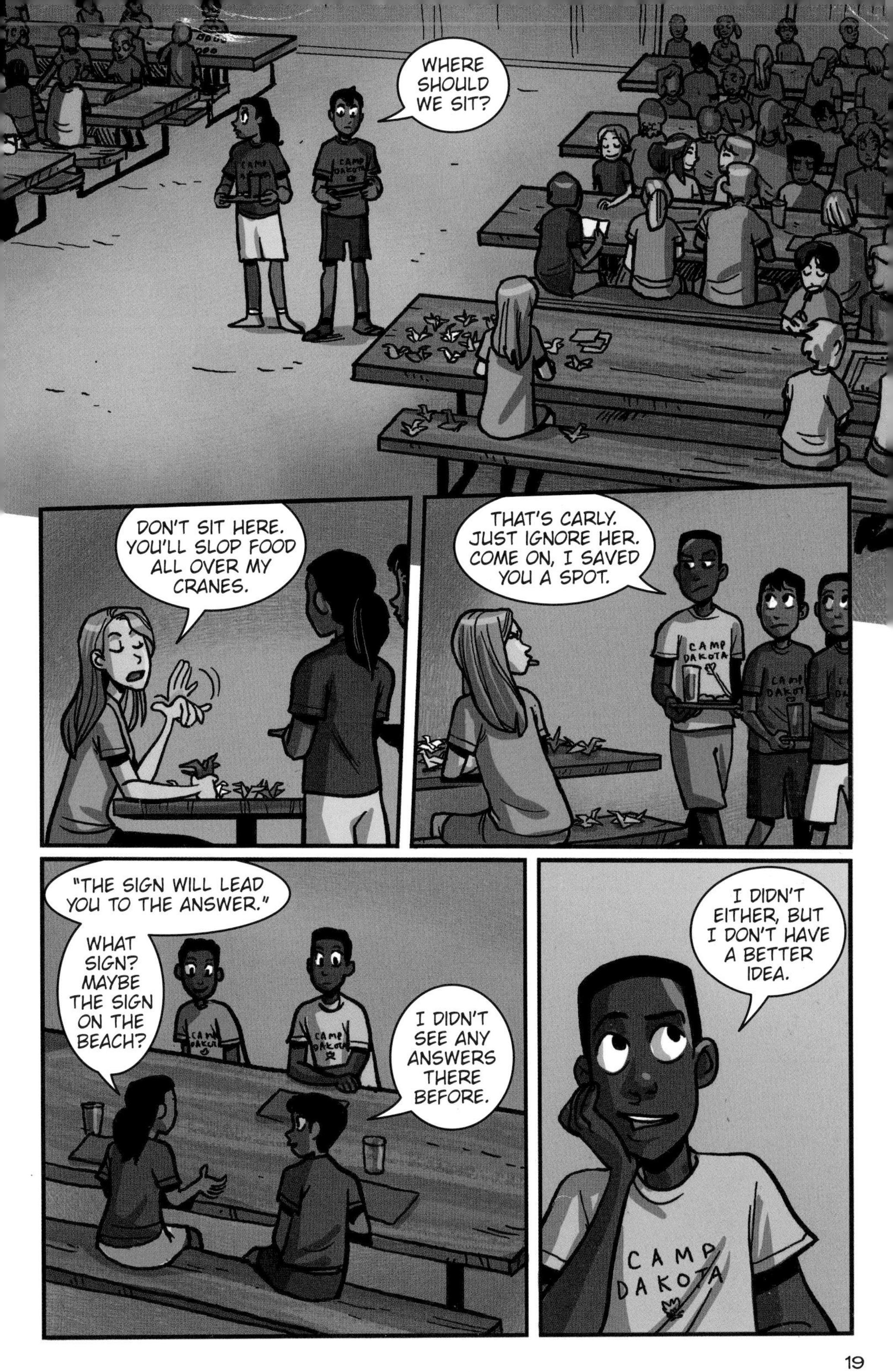
WHERE SHOULD WE SIT?
DON'T SIT HERE. YOU'LL SLOP FOOD ALL OVER MY CRANES.
THAT'S CARLY. JUST IGNORE HER. COME ON, I SAVED YOU A SPOT.
CAMP DAKOTA
"THE SIGN WILL LEAD YOU TO THE ANSWER."
WHAT SIGN? MAYBE THE SIGN ON THE BEACH?
I DIDN'T SEE ANY ANSWERS THERE BEFORE.
I DIDN'T EITHER, BUT I DON'T HAVE A BETTER IDEA.
CAMP DAKOTA

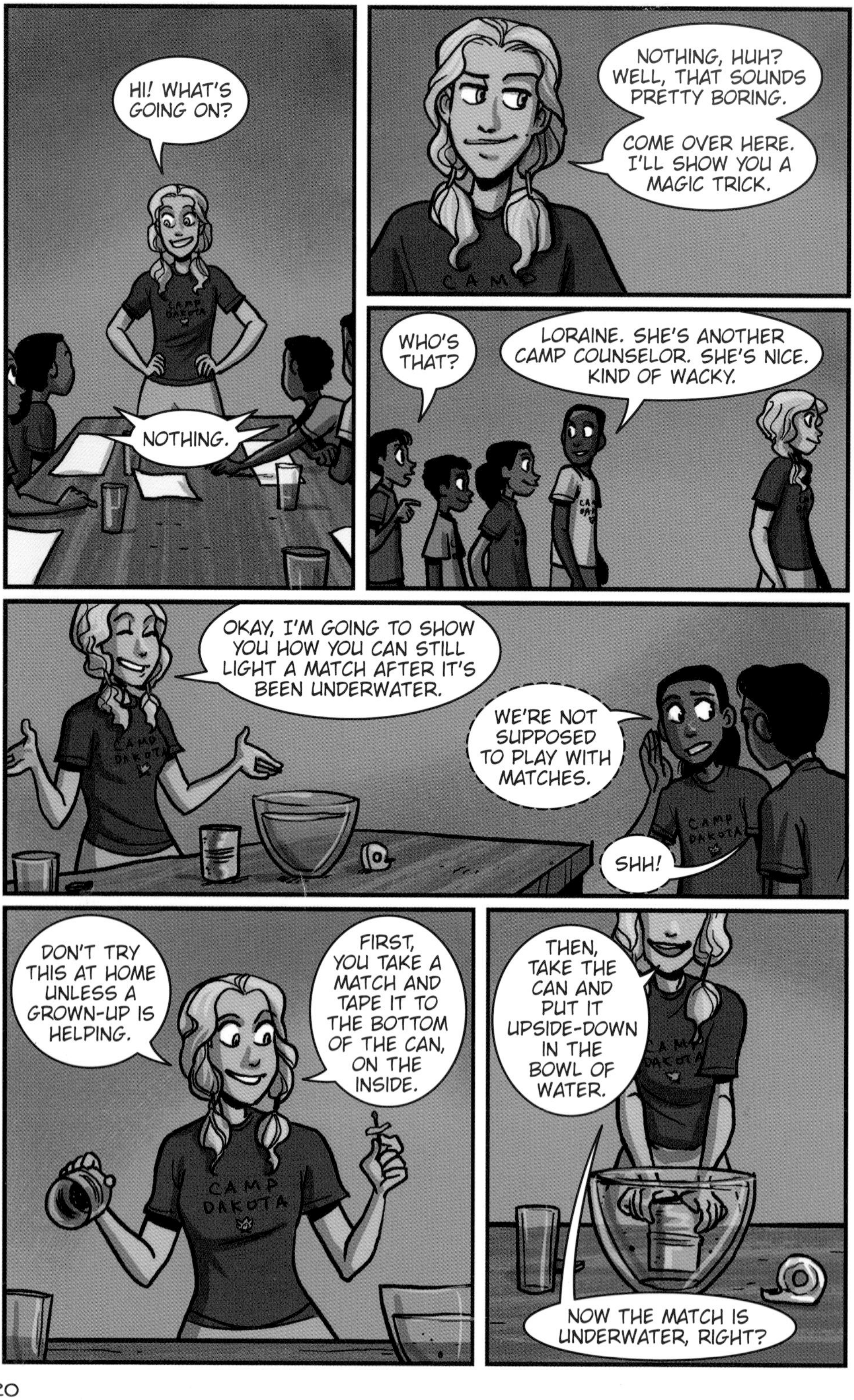
HI! WHAT'S GOING ON?
NOTHING.
NOTHING, HUH? WELL, THAT SOUNDS PRETTY BORING.
COME OVER HERE. I'LL SHOW YOU A MAGIC TRICK.
WHO'S THAT?
LORAINE. SHE'S ANOTHER CAMP COUNSELOR. SHE'S NICE. KIND OF WACKY.
OKAY, I'M GOING TO SHOW YOU HOW YOU CAN STILL LIGHT A MATCH AFTER IT'S BEEN UNDERWATER.
WE'RE NOT SUPPOSED TO PLAY WITH MATCHES.
SHH!
DON'T TRY THIS AT HOME UNLESS A GROWN-UP IS HELPING.
FIRST, YOU TAKE A MATCH AND TAPE IT TO THE BOTTOM OF THE CAN, ON THE INSIDE.
THEN, TAKE THE CAN AND PUT IT UPSIDE-DOWN IN THE BOWL OF WATER.
NOW THE MATCH IS UNDERWATER, RIGHT?

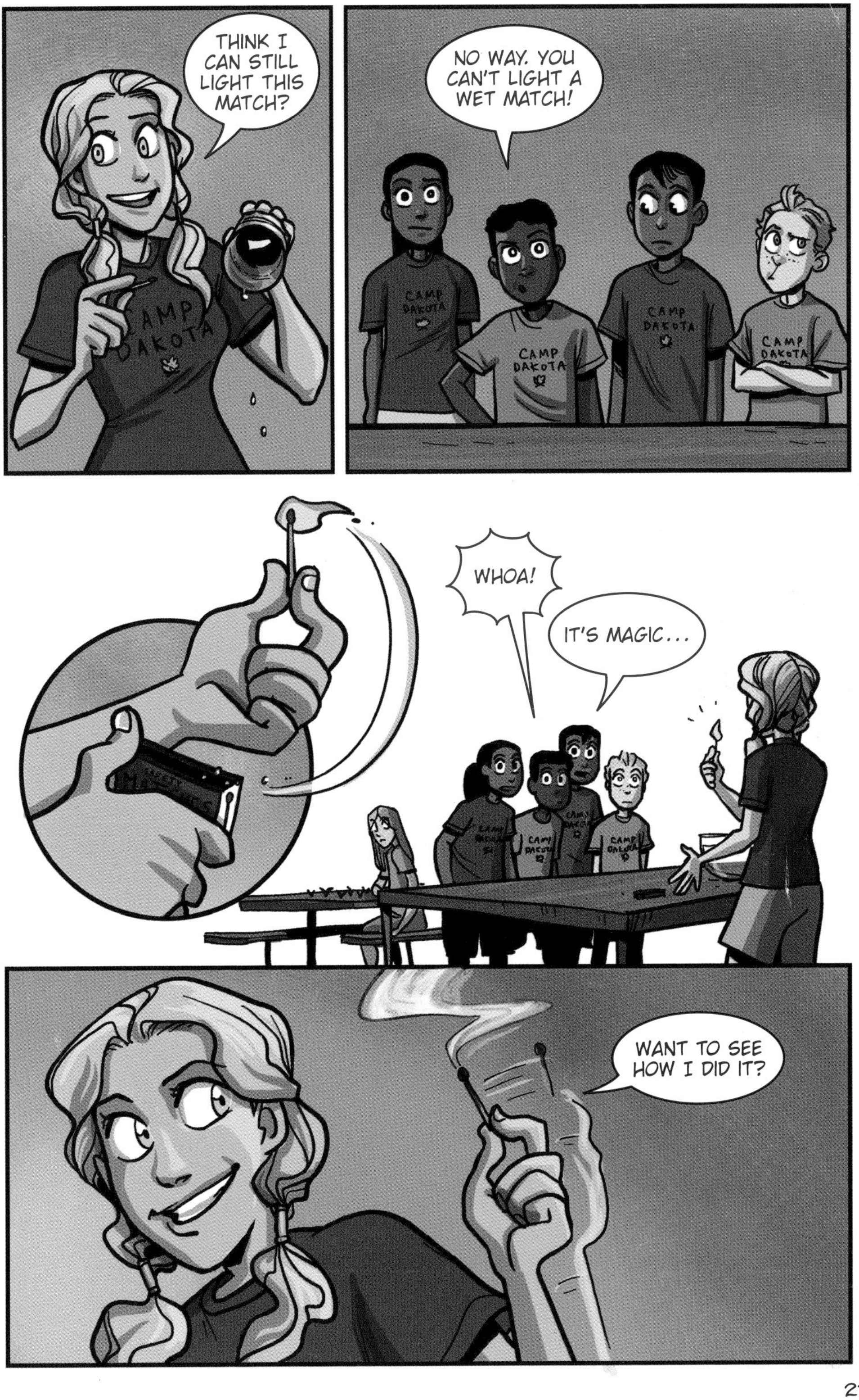
THINK I CAN STILL LIGHT THIS MATCH?
NO WAY. YOU CAN'T LIGHT A WET MATCH!
SAFETY MATCHES
WHOA!
IT'S MAGIC...
WANT TO SEE HOW I DID IT?

LET'S TRY THIS AGAIN, WITH A CLEAR GLASS THIS TIME, SO YOU CAN SEE WHAT HAPPENS.

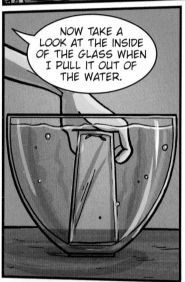

NOW TAKE A LOOK AT THE INSIDE OF THE GLASS WHEN I PULL IT OUT OF THE WATER.

IT LOOKS LIKE ONLY THE BOTTOM OF THE GLASS GOT WET ON THE INSIDE.

SO THE MATCH STAYED DRY?

THAT'S RIGHT! DOES ANYONE KNOW WHY?

I DON'T GET IT. THE GLASS WAS EMPTY.

SO WHY DIDN'T THE WATER GO IN?

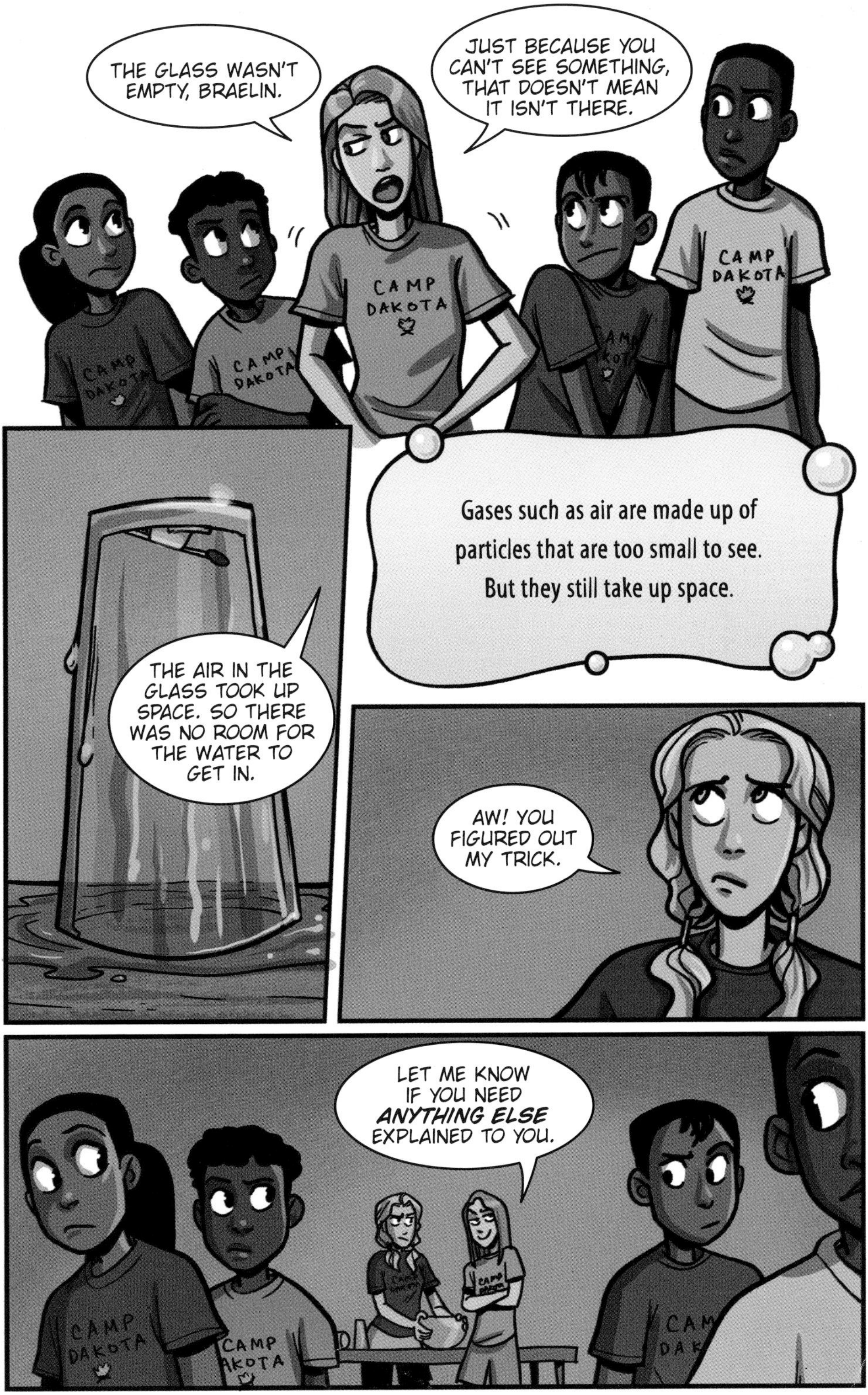
THE GLASS WASN'T EMPTY, BRAELIN.
JUST BECAUSE YOU CAN'T SEE SOMETHING, THAT DOESN'T MEAN IT ISN'T THERE.
CAMP DAKOTA
Gases such as air are made up of particles that are too small to see. But they still take up space.
THE AIR IN THE GLASS TOOK UP SPACE. SO THERE WAS NO ROOM FOR THE WATER TO GET IN.
AW! YOU FIGURED OUT MY TRICK.
LET ME KNOW IF YOU NEED ***ANYTHING ELSE*** EXPLAINED TO YOU.

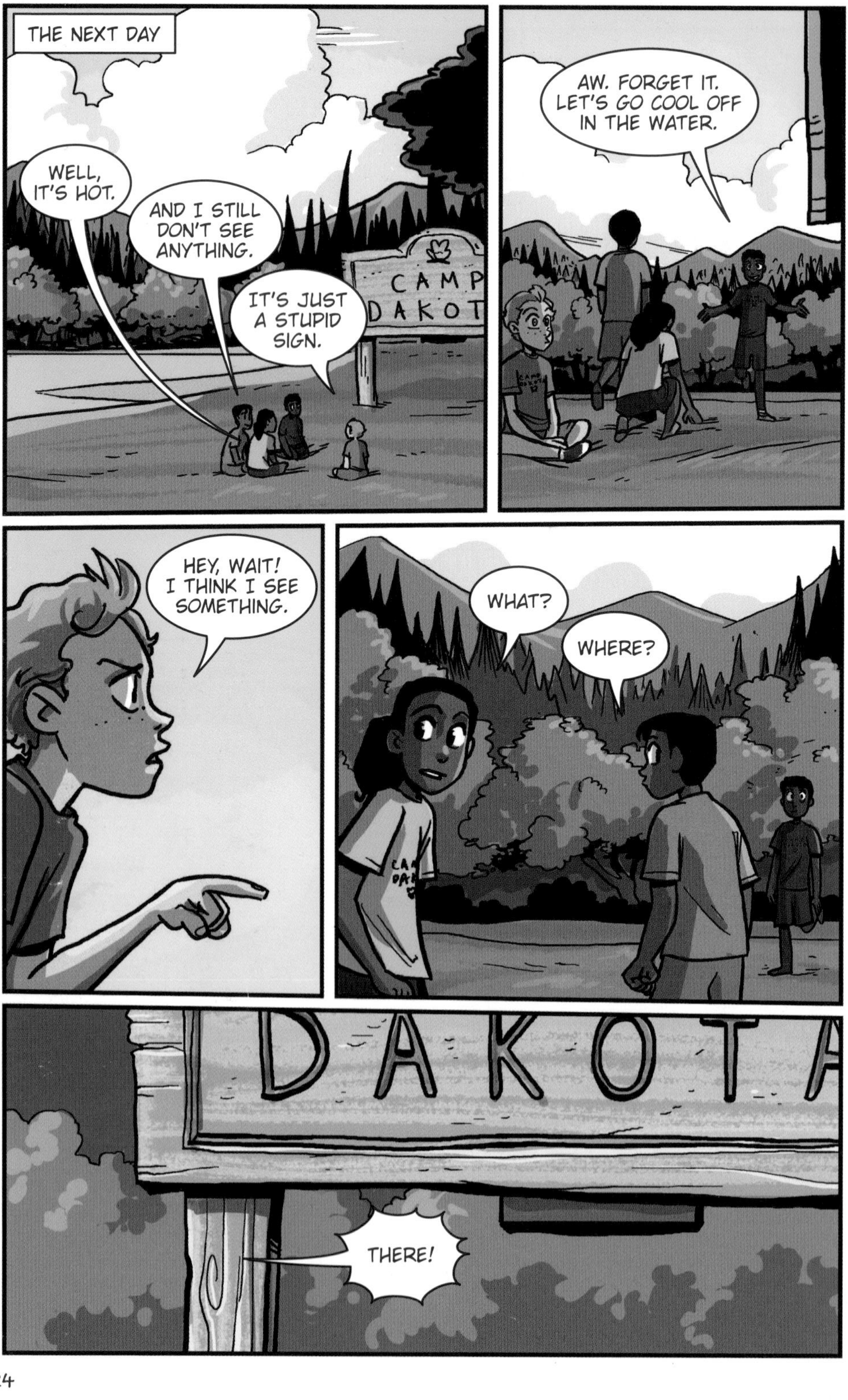
THE NEXT DAY
WELL, IT'S HOT.
AND I STILL DON'T SEE ANYTHING.
CAMP DAKOT
IT'S JUST A STUPID SIGN.
AW. FORGET IT. LET'S GO COOL OFF IN THE WATER.
HEY, WAIT! I THINK I SEE SOMETHING.
WHAT?
WHERE?
DAKOTA
THERE!

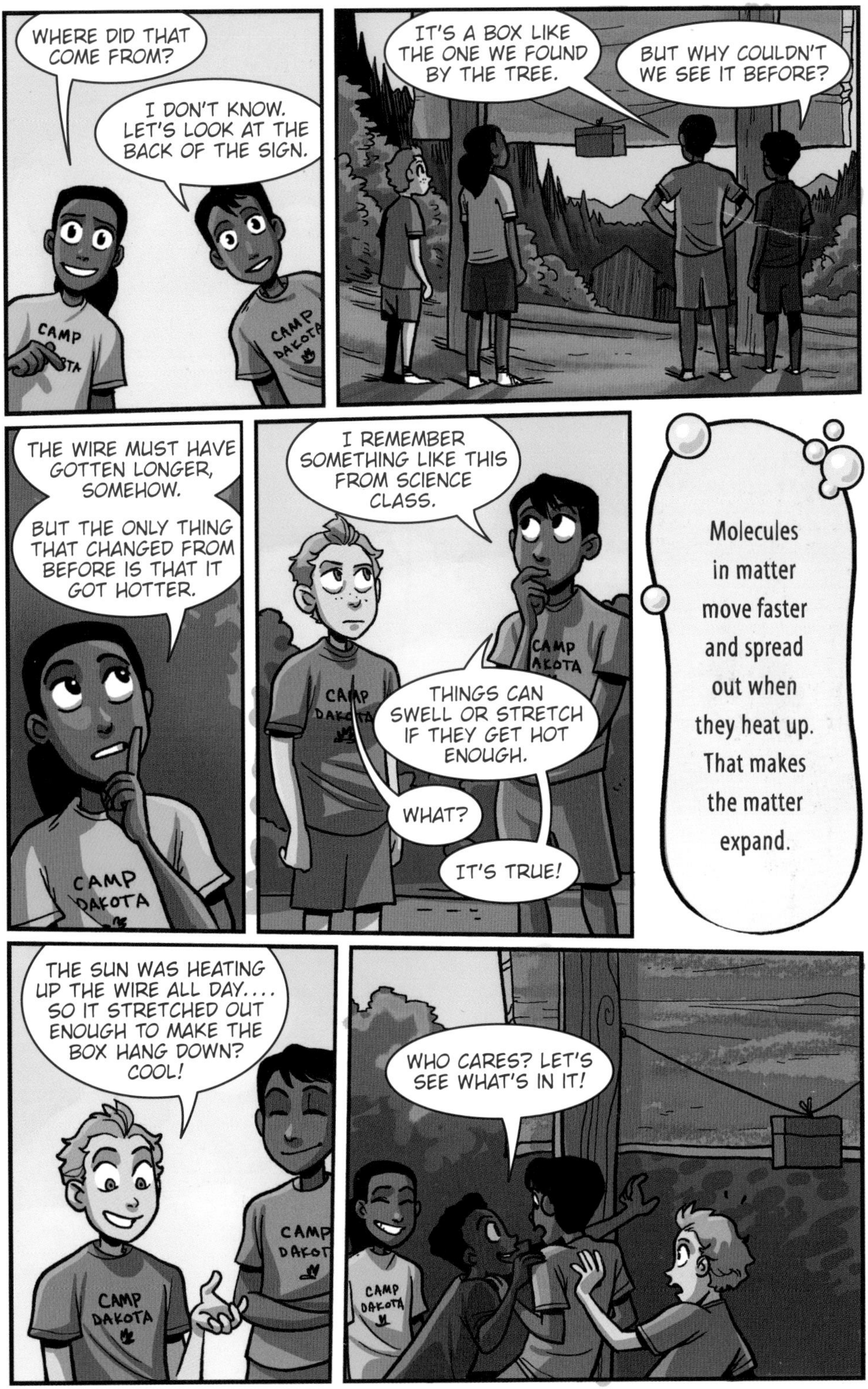
WHERE DID THAT COME FROM?
I DON'T KNOW. LET'S LOOK AT THE BACK OF THE SIGN.
IT'S A BOX LIKE THE ONE WE FOUND BY THE TREE.
BUT WHY COULDN'T WE SEE IT BEFORE?
THE WIRE MUST HAVE GOTTEN LONGER, SOMEHOW.
BUT THE ONLY THING THAT CHANGED FROM BEFORE IS THAT IT GOT HOTTER.
I REMEMBER SOMETHING LIKE THIS FROM SCIENCE CLASS.
THINGS CAN SWELL OR STRETCH IF THEY GET HOT ENOUGH.
WHAT?
IT'S TRUE!
Molecules in matter move faster and spread out when they heat up. That makes the matter expand.
THE SUN WAS HEATING UP THE WIRE ALL DAY.... SO IT STRETCHED OUT ENOUGH TO MAKE THE BOX HANG DOWN? COOL!
WHO CARES? LET'S SEE WHAT'S IN IT!

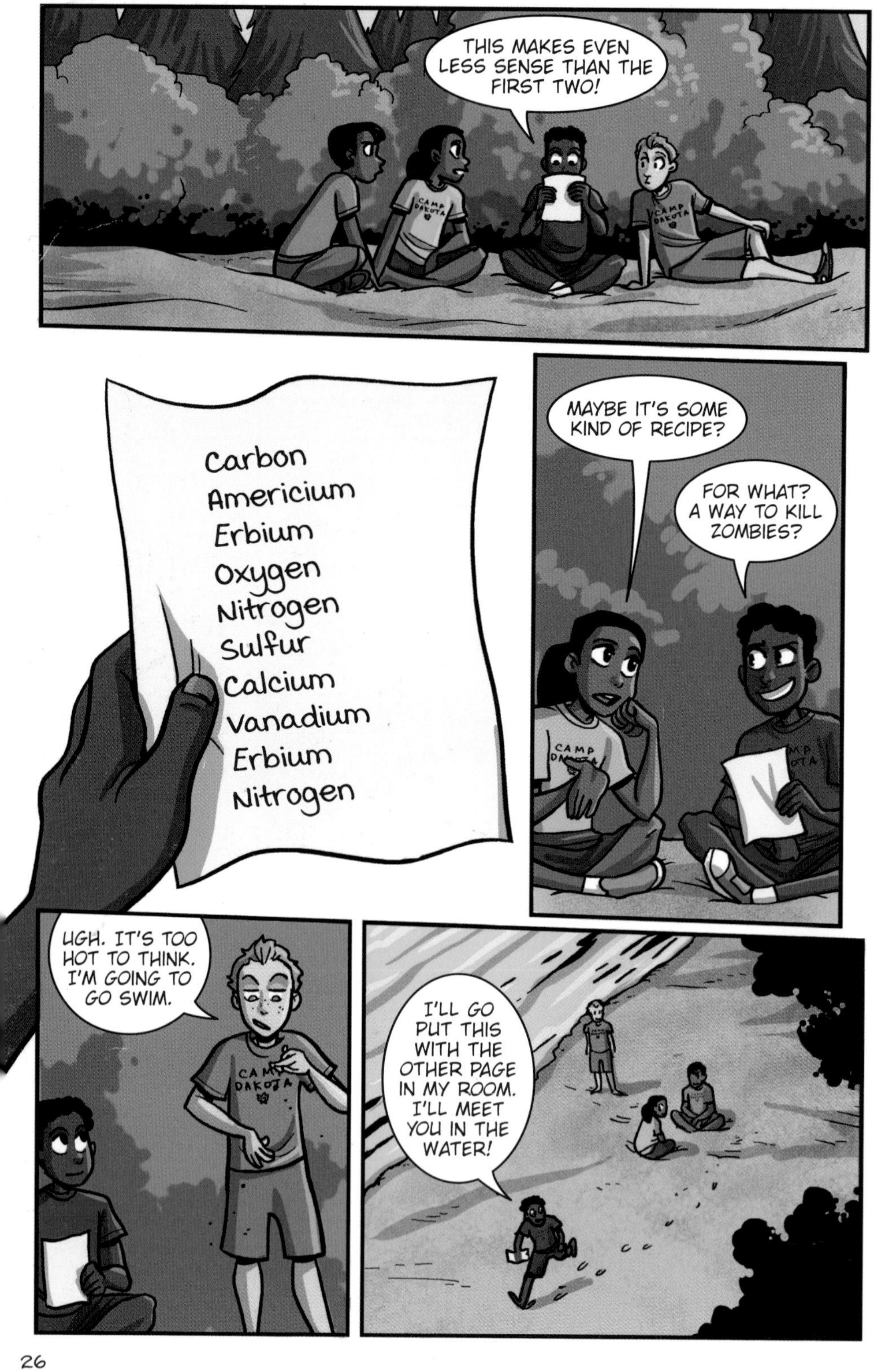
THIS MAKES EVEN LESS SENSE THAN THE FIRST TWO!
Carbon
Americium
Erbium
Oxygen
Nitrogen
Sulfur
Calcium
Vanadium
Erbium
Nitrogen
MAYBE IT'S SOME KIND OF RECIPE?
FOR WHAT? A WAY TO KILL ZOMBIES?
UGH. IT'S TOO HOT TO THINK. I'M GOING TO GO SWIM.
I'LL GO PUT THIS WITH THE OTHER PAGE IN MY ROOM. I'LL MEET YOU IN THE WATER!

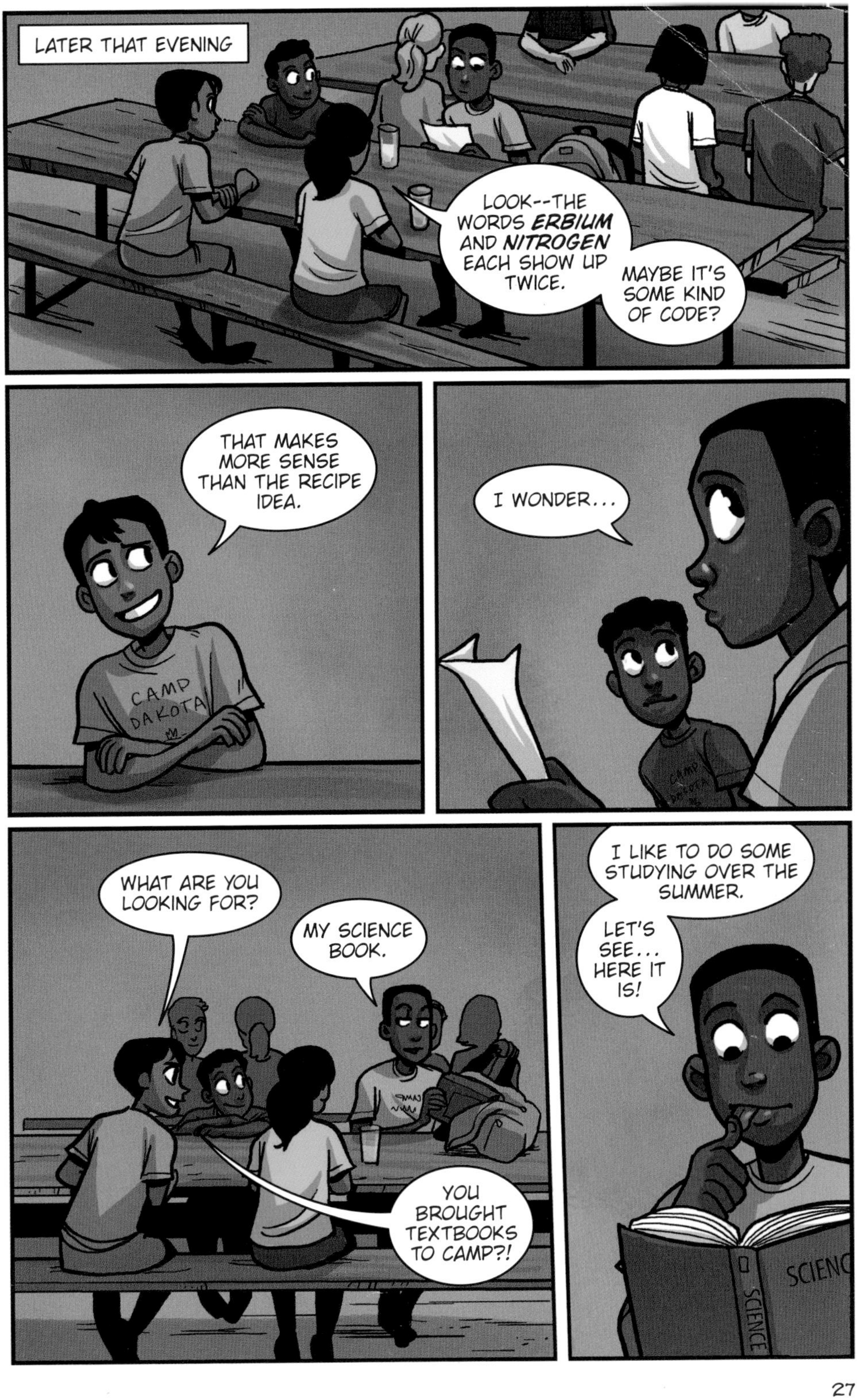
LATER THAT EVENING
LOOK--THE WORDS **ERBIUM** AND **NITROGEN** EACH SHOW UP TWICE.
MAYBE IT'S SOME KIND OF CODE?
THAT MAKES MORE SENSE THAN THE RECIPE IDEA.
CAMP DAKOTA
I WONDER...
WHAT ARE YOU LOOKING FOR?
MY SCIENCE BOOK.
YOU BROUGHT TEXTBOOKS TO CAMP?!
I LIKE TO DO SOME STUDYING OVER THE SUMMER.
LET'S SEE... HERE IT IS!
SCIENCE

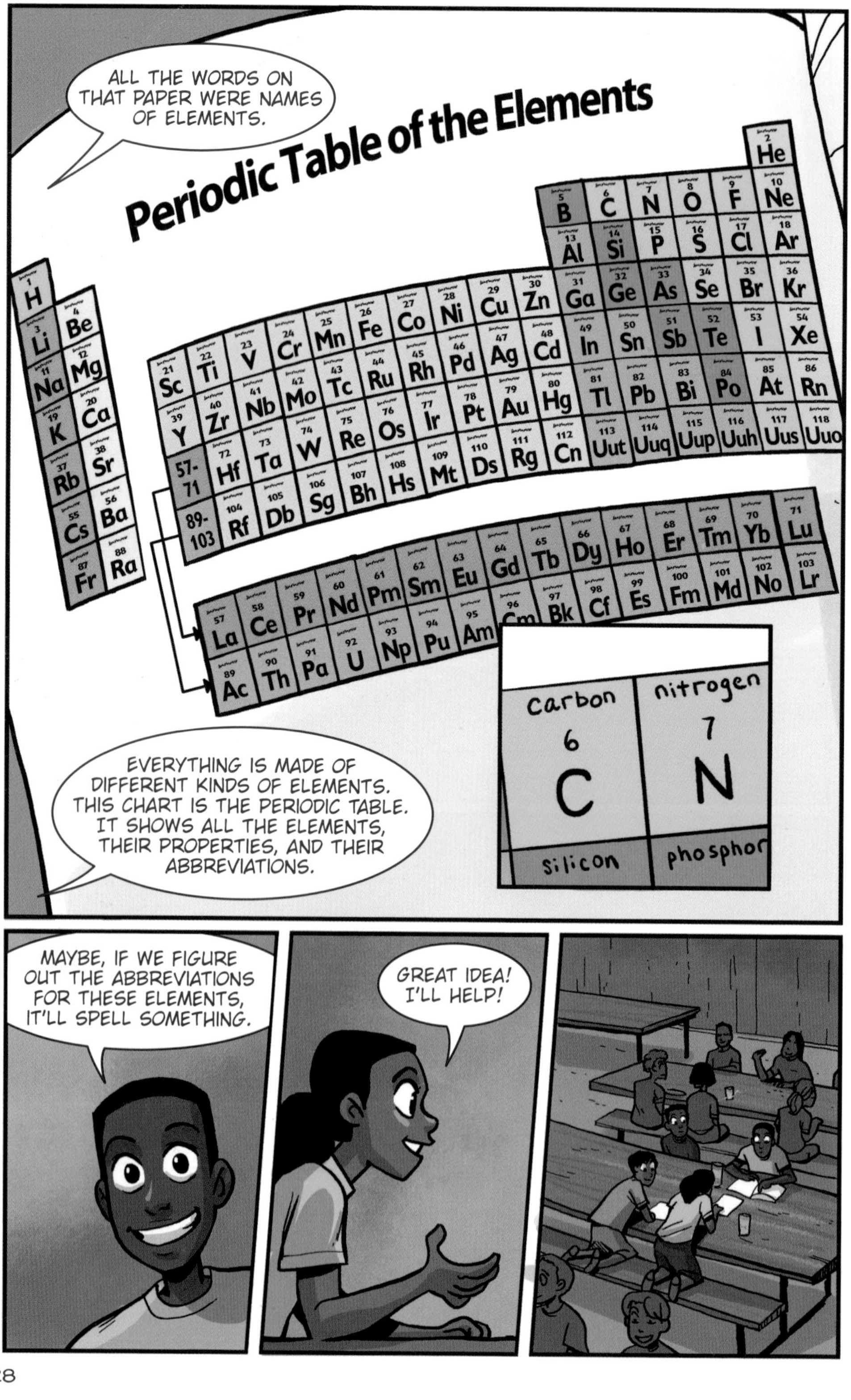
ALL THE WORDS ON THAT PAPER WERE NAMES OF ELEMENTS.
Periodic Table of the Elements
carbon
6
C
nitrogen
7
N
silicon
phosphor
EVERYTHING IS MADE OF DIFFERENT KINDS OF ELEMENTS. THIS CHART IS THE PERIODIC TABLE. IT SHOWS ALL THE ELEMENTS, THEIR PROPERTIES, AND THEIR ABBREVIATIONS.
MAYBE, IF WE FIGURE OUT THE ABBREVIATIONS FOR THESE ELEMENTS, IT'LL SPELL SOMETHING.
GREAT IDEA! I'LL HELP!

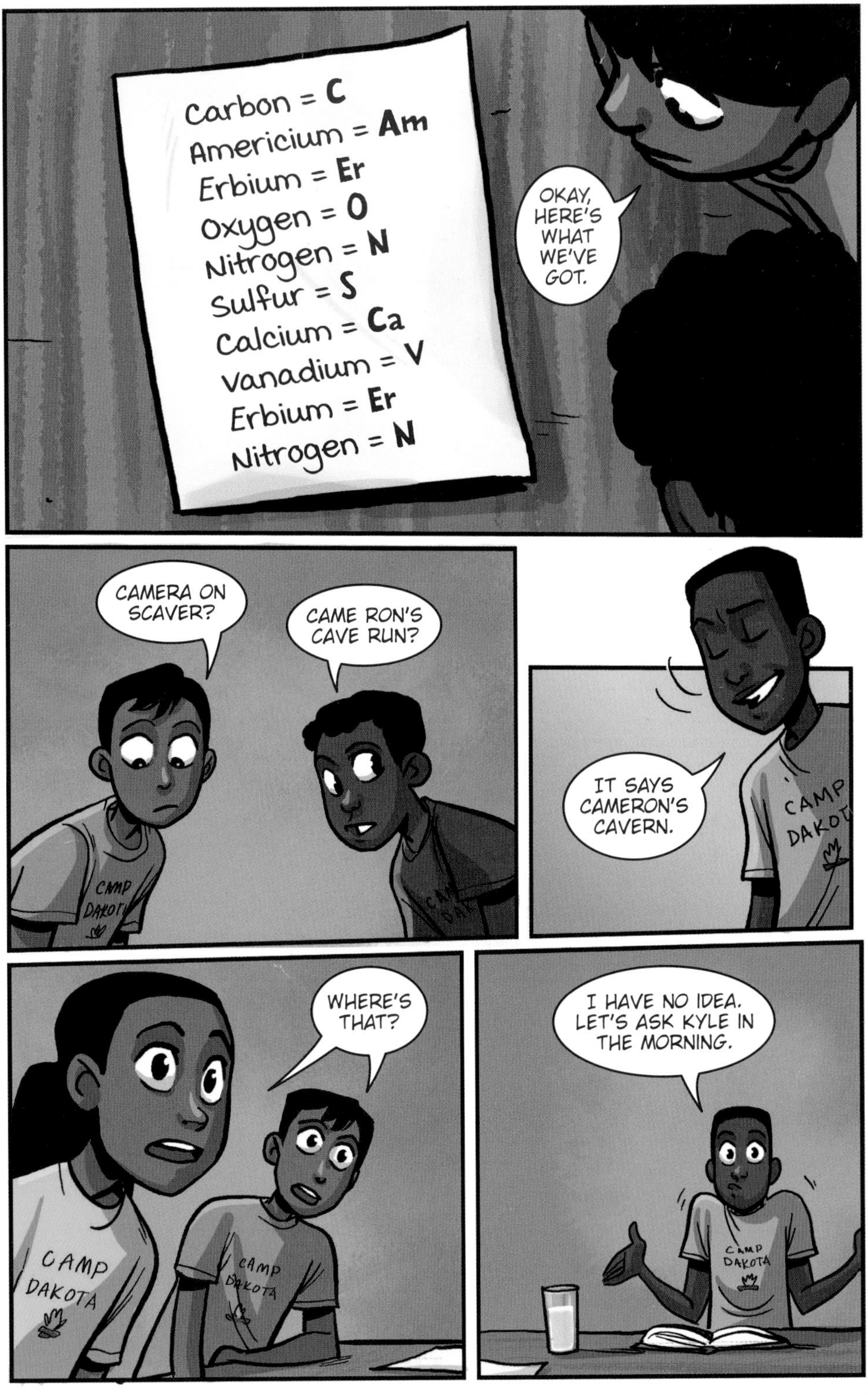
Carbon = C
Americium = Am
Erbium = Er
Oxygen = O
Nitrogen = N
Sulfur = S
Calcium = Ca
Vanadium = V
Erbium = Er
Nitrogen = N
OKAY, HERE'S WHAT WE'VE GOT.
CAMERA ON SCAVER?
CAME RON'S CAVE RUN?
IT SAYS CAMERON'S CAVERN.
WHERE'S THAT?
I HAVE NO IDEA. LET'S ASK KYLE IN THE MORNING.

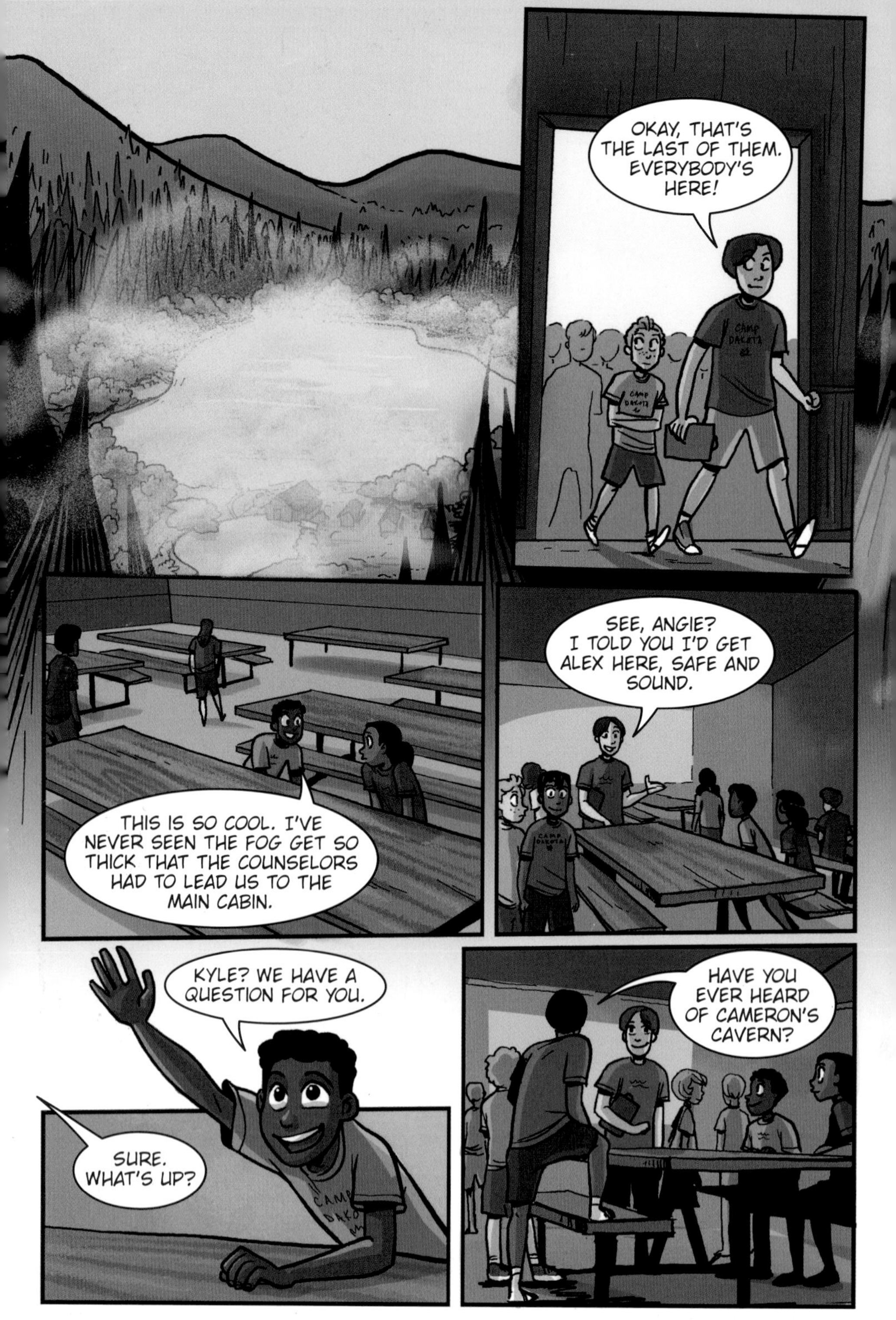
OKAY, THAT'S THE LAST OF THEM. EVERYBODY'S HERE!
THIS IS SO COOL. I'VE NEVER SEEN THE FOG GET SO THICK THAT THE COUNSELORS HAD TO LEAD US TO THE MAIN CABIN.
SEE, ANGIE? I TOLD YOU I'D GET ALEX HERE, SAFE AND SOUND.
KYLE? WE HAVE A QUESTION FOR YOU.
SURE. WHAT'S UP?
HAVE YOU EVER HEARD OF CAMERON'S CAVERN?

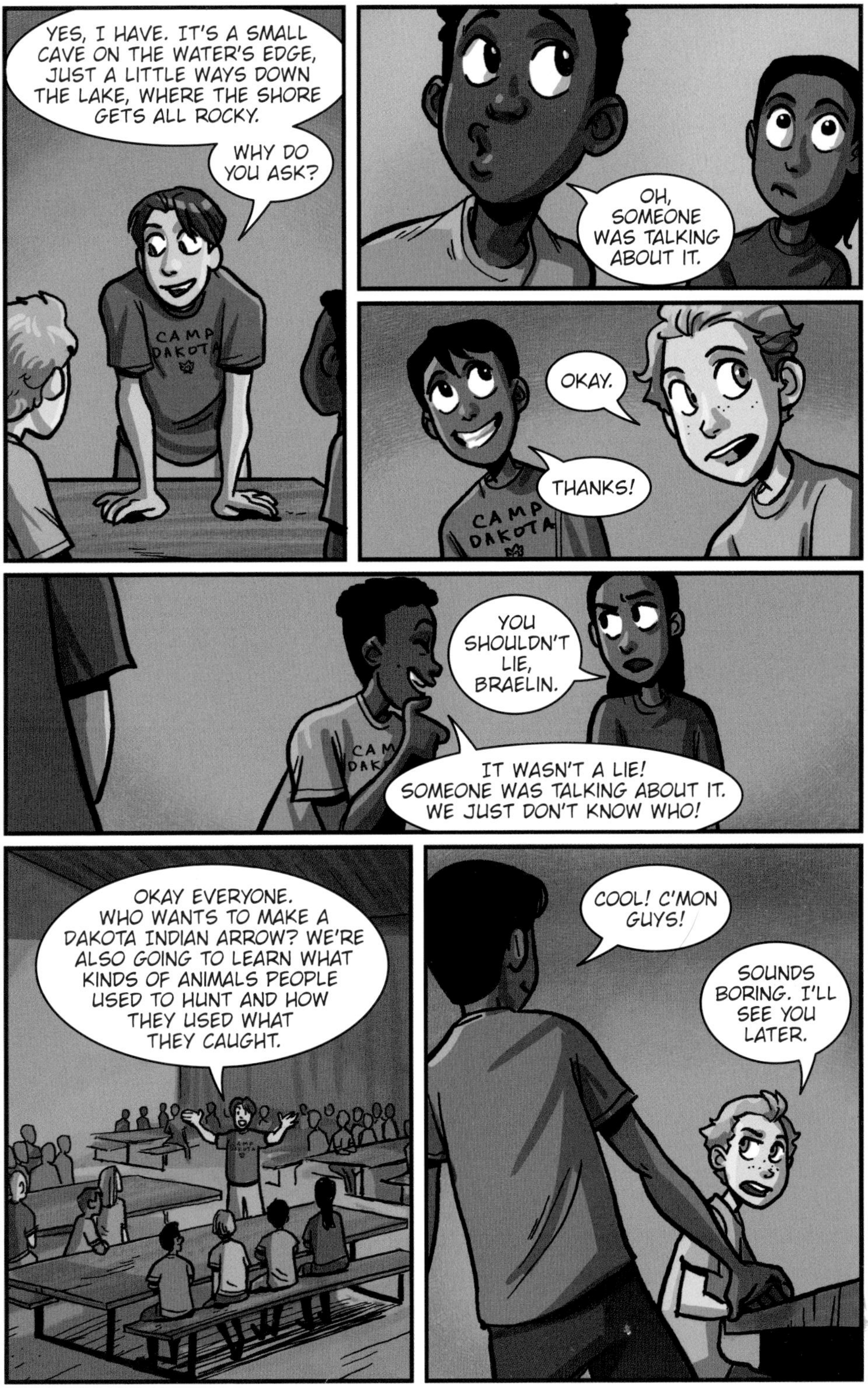
YES, I HAVE. IT'S A SMALL CAVE ON THE WATER'S EDGE, JUST A LITTLE WAYS DOWN THE LAKE, WHERE THE SHORE GETS ALL ROCKY.
WHY DO YOU ASK?
CAMP DAKOTA
OH, SOMEONE WAS TALKING ABOUT IT.
OKAY.
THANKS!
CAMP DAKOTA
YOU SHOULDN'T LIE, BRAELIN.
IT WASN'T A LIE! SOMEONE WAS TALKING ABOUT IT. WE JUST DON'T KNOW WHO!
OKAY EVERYONE. WHO WANTS TO MAKE A DAKOTA INDIAN ARROW? WE'RE ALSO GOING TO LEARN WHAT KINDS OF ANIMALS PEOPLE USED TO HUNT AND HOW THEY USED WHAT THEY CAUGHT.
COOL! C'MON GUYS!
SOUNDS BORING. I'LL SEE YOU LATER.

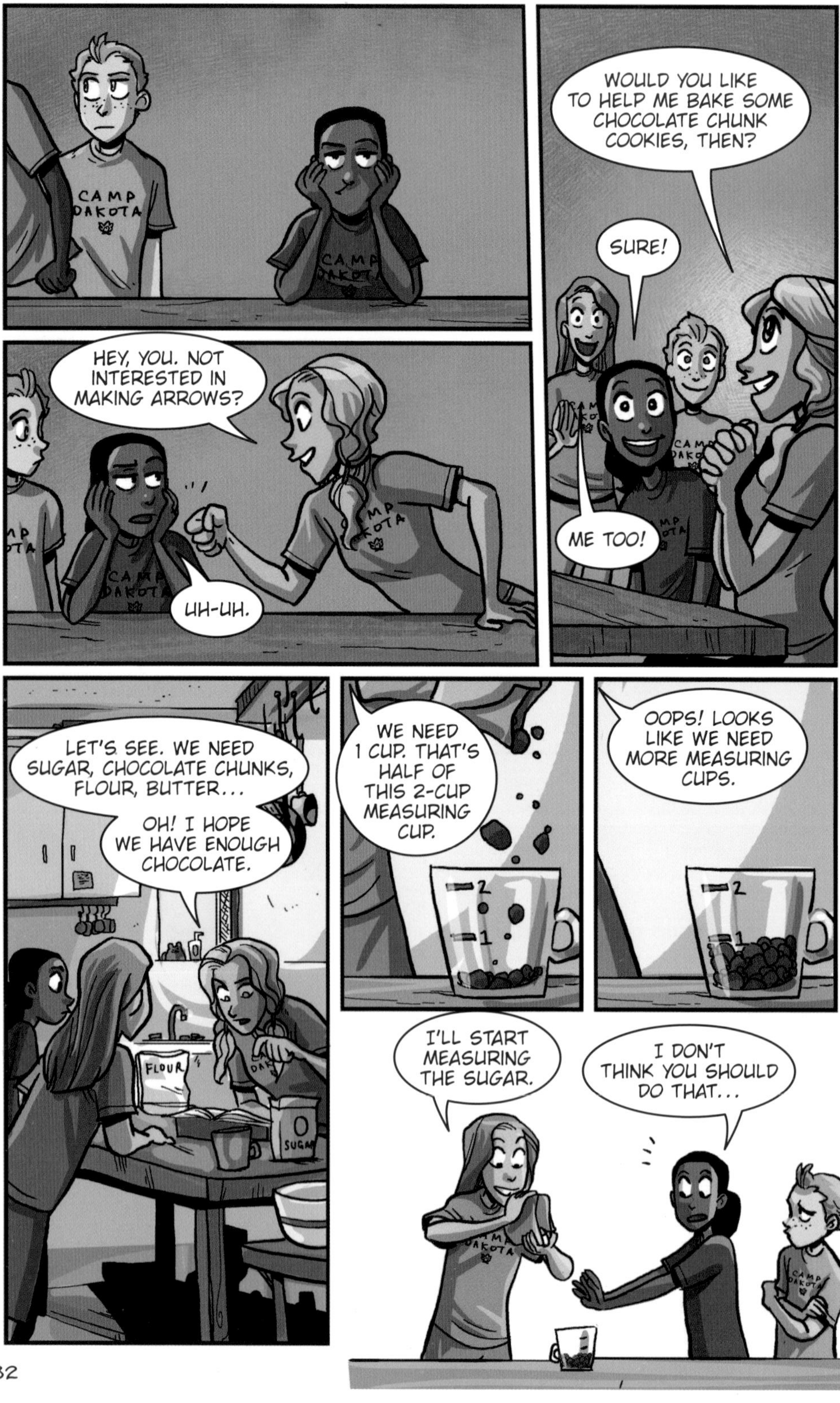
CAMP DAKOTA
HEY, YOU. NOT INTERESTED IN MAKING ARROWS?
UH-UH.
WOULD YOU LIKE TO HELP ME BAKE SOME CHOCOLATE CHUNK COOKIES, THEN?
SURE!
ME TOO!
LET'S SEE. WE NEED SUGAR, CHOCOLATE CHUNKS, FLOUR, BUTTER...
OH! I HOPE WE HAVE ENOUGH CHOCOLATE.
FLOUR
SUGAR
WE NEED 1 CUP. THAT'S HALF OF THIS 2-CUP MEASURING CUP.
OOPS! LOOKS LIKE WE NEED MORE MEASURING CUPS.
I'LL START MEASURING THE SUGAR.
I DON'T THINK YOU SHOULD DO THAT...

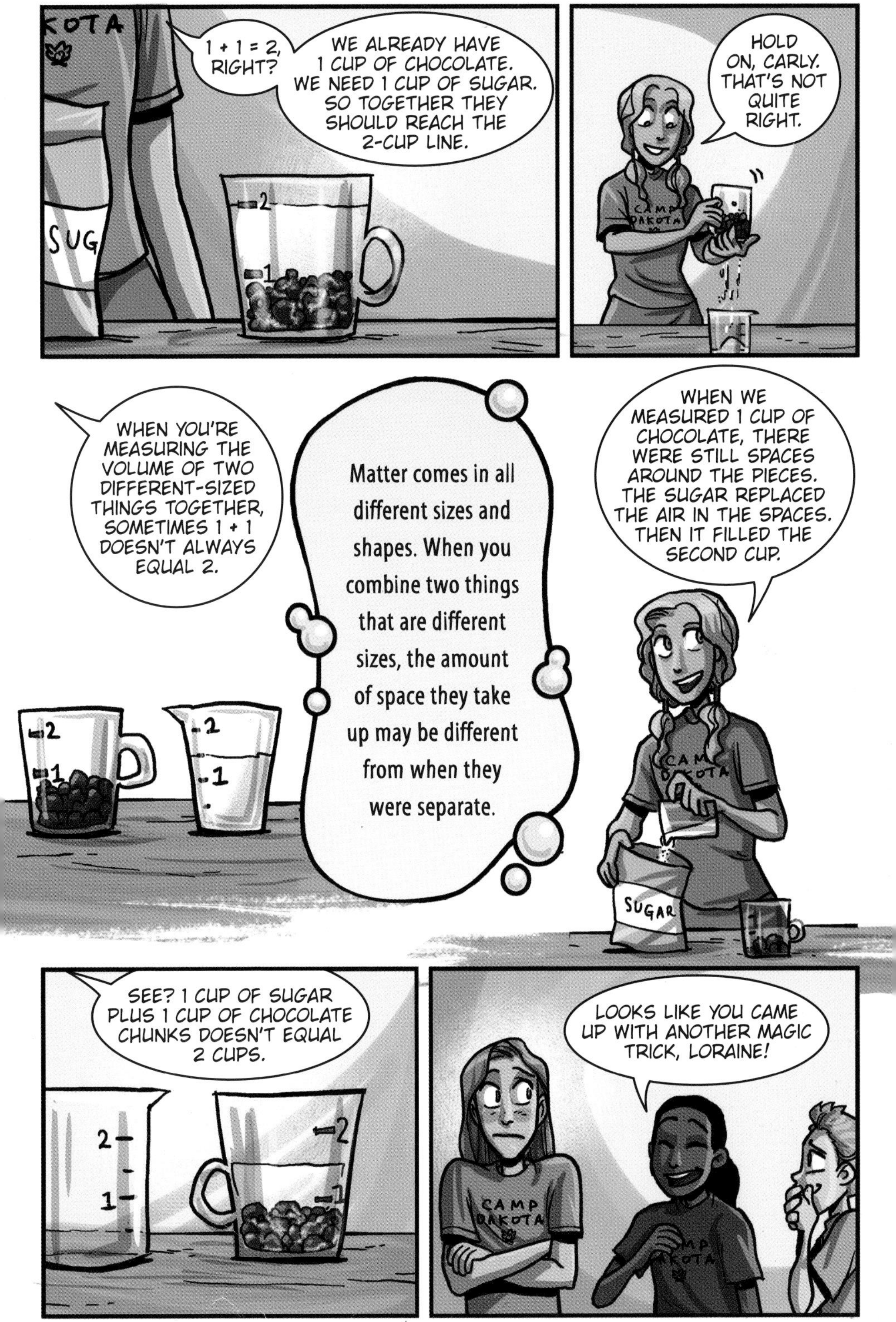
KOTA
SUG
1 + 1 = 2, RIGHT?
WE ALREADY HAVE 1 CUP OF CHOCOLATE. WE NEED 1 CUP OF SUGAR. SO TOGETHER THEY SHOULD REACH THE 2-CUP LINE.
HOLD ON, CARLY. THAT'S NOT QUITE RIGHT.
WHEN YOU'RE MEASURING THE VOLUME OF TWO DIFFERENT-SIZED THINGS TOGETHER, SOMETIMES 1 + 1 DOESN'T ALWAYS EQUAL 2.
Matter comes in all different sizes and shapes. When you combine two things that are different sizes, the amount of space they take up may be different from when they were separate.
WHEN WE MEASURED 1 CUP OF CHOCOLATE, THERE WERE STILL SPACES AROUND THE PIECES. THE SUGAR REPLACED THE AIR IN THE SPACES. THEN IT FILLED THE SECOND CUP.
SUGAR
SEE? 1 CUP OF SUGAR PLUS 1 CUP OF CHOCOLATE CHUNKS DOESN'T EQUAL 2 CUPS.
LOOKS LIKE YOU CAME UP WITH ANOTHER MAGIC TRICK, LORAINE!

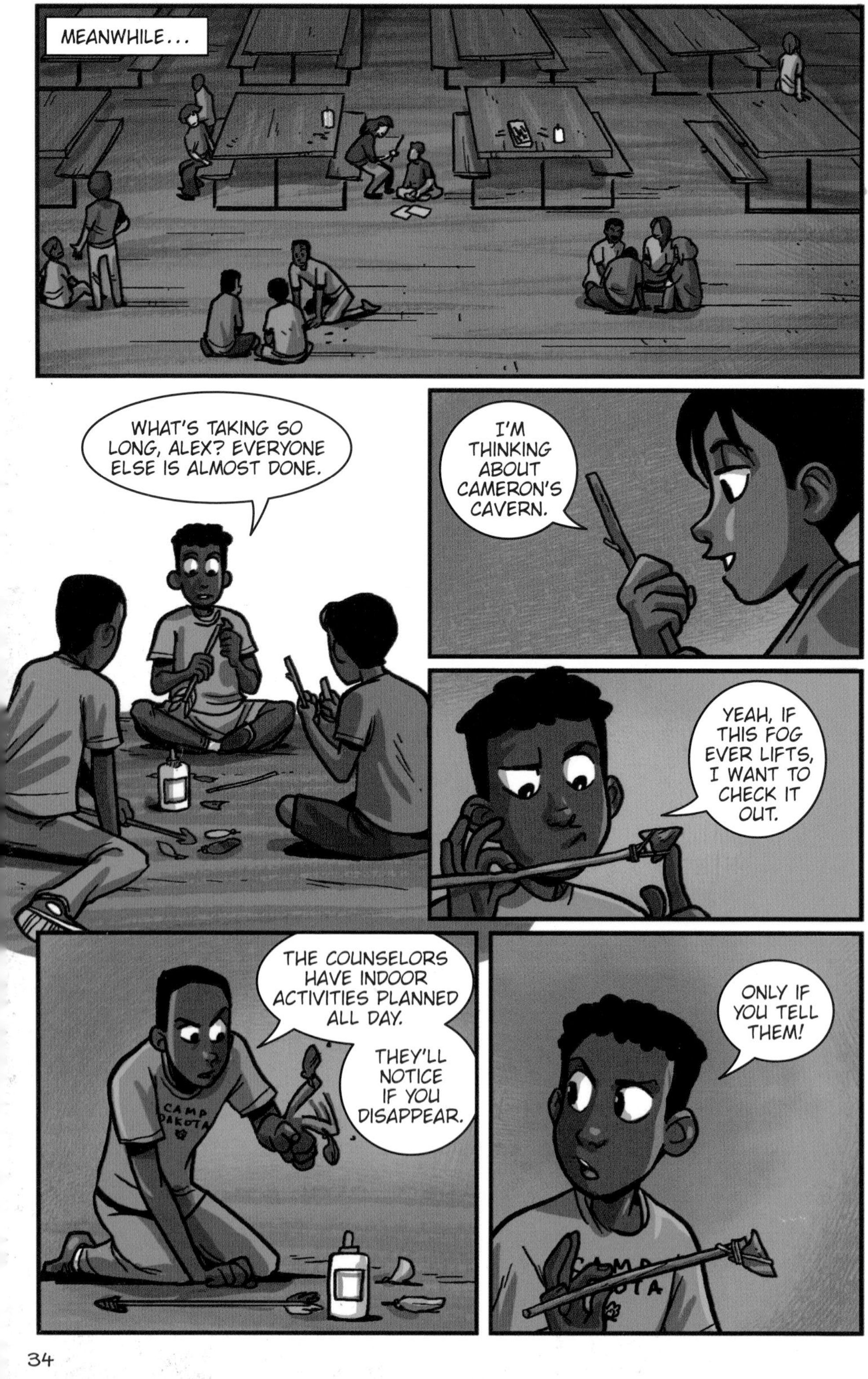
MEANWHILE...
WHAT'S TAKING SO LONG, ALEX? EVERYONE ELSE IS ALMOST DONE.
I'M THINKING ABOUT CAMERON'S CAVERN.
YEAH, IF THIS FOG EVER LIFTS, I WANT TO CHECK IT OUT.
THE COUNSELORS HAVE INDOOR ACTIVITIES PLANNED ALL DAY.
THEY'LL NOTICE IF YOU DISAPPEAR.
ONLY IF YOU TELL THEM!

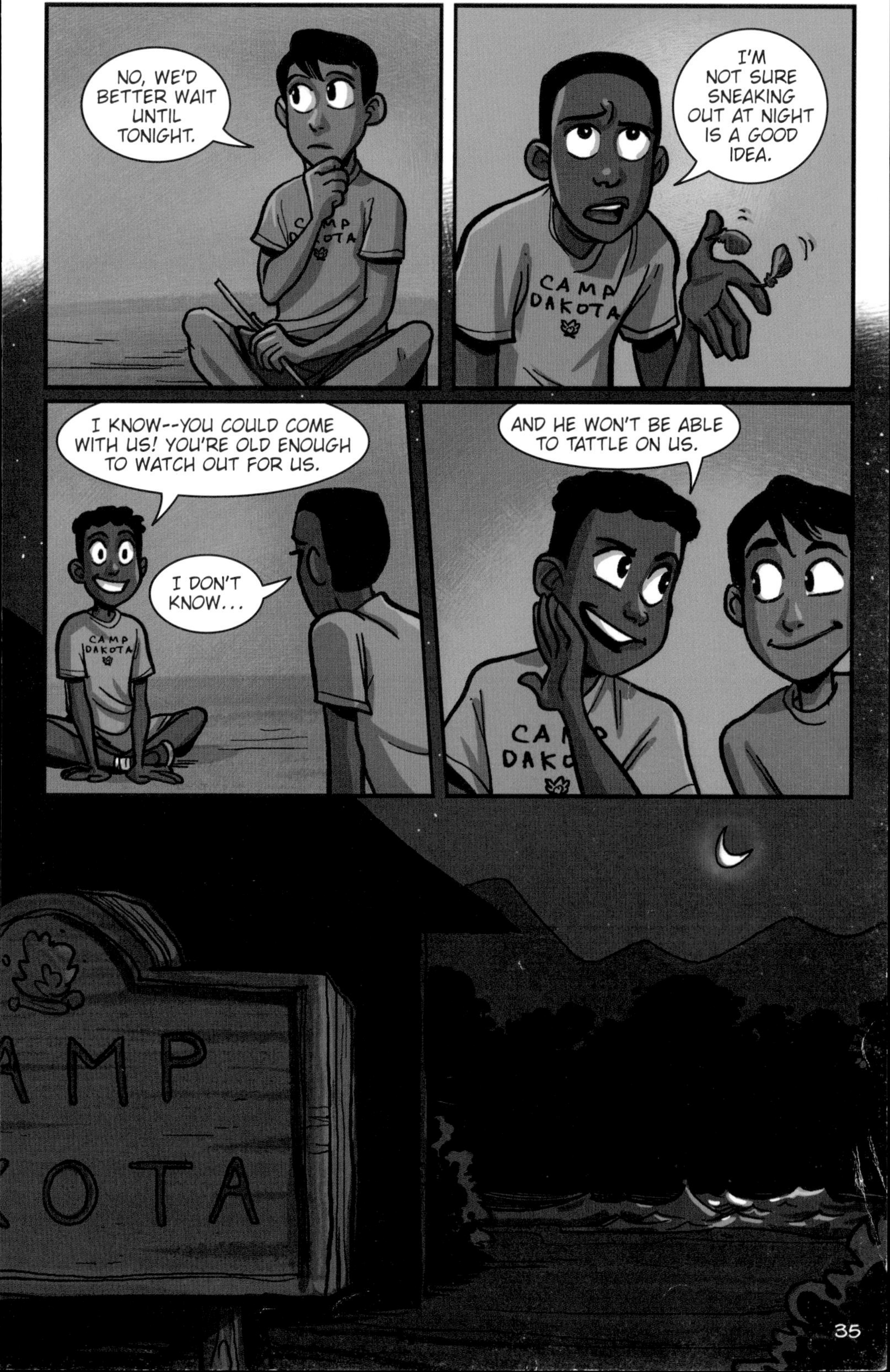
NO, WE'D BETTER WAIT UNTIL TONIGHT.
CAMP DAKOTA
I'M NOT SURE SNEAKING OUT AT NIGHT IS A GOOD IDEA.
CAMP DAKOTA
I KNOW--YOU COULD COME WITH US! YOU'RE OLD ENOUGH TO WATCH OUT FOR US.
CAMP DAKOTA
I DON'T KNOW...
AND HE WON'T BE ABLE TO TATTLE ON US.
CAMP DAKO
AMP
OTA

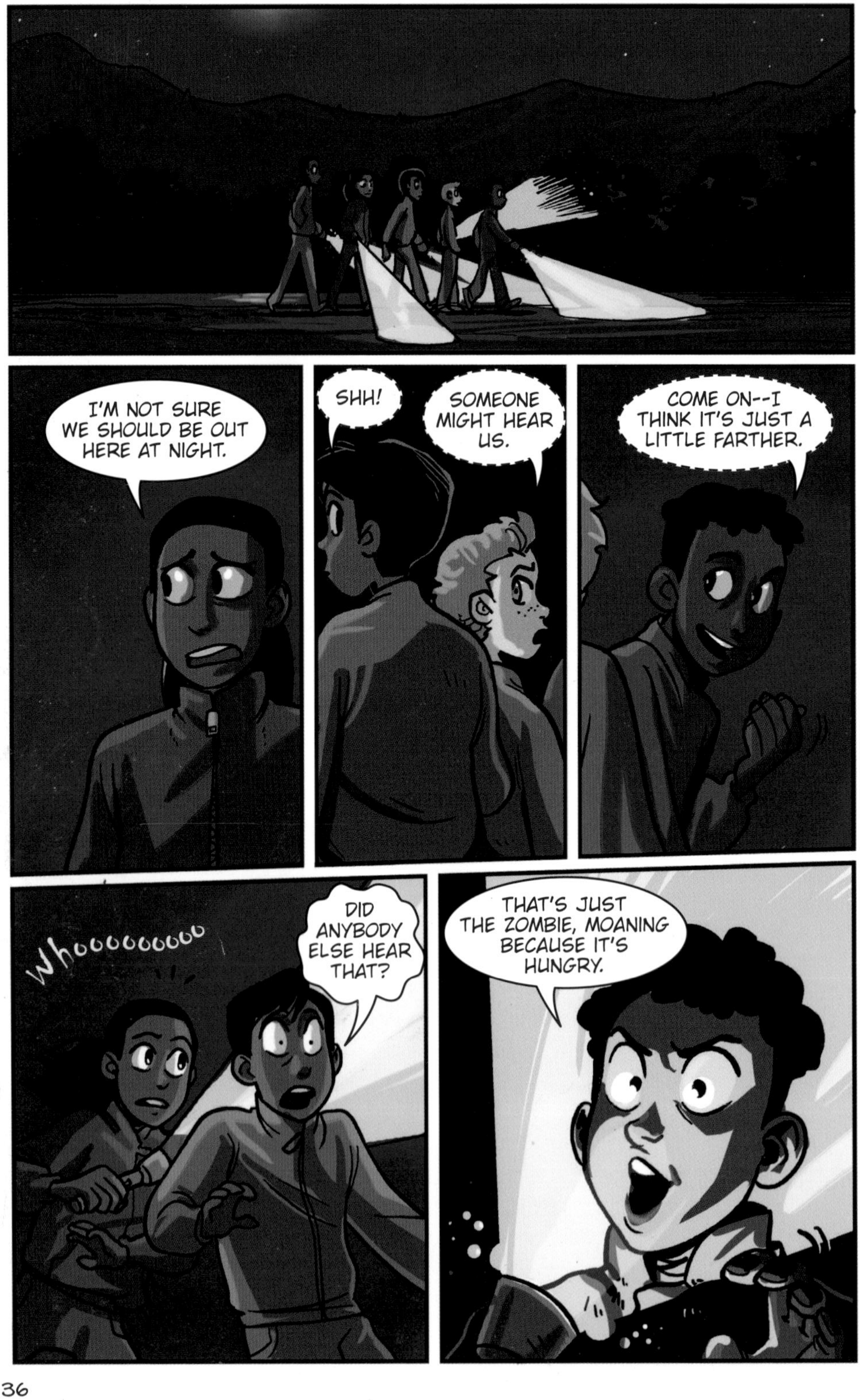
I'M NOT SURE WE SHOULD BE OUT HERE AT NIGHT.
SHH!
SOMEONE MIGHT HEAR US.
COME ON--I THINK IT'S JUST A LITTLE FARTHER.
Whoooooooooo
DID ANYBODY ELSE HEAR THAT?
THAT'S JUST THE ZOMBIE, MOANING BECAUSE IT'S HUNGRY.

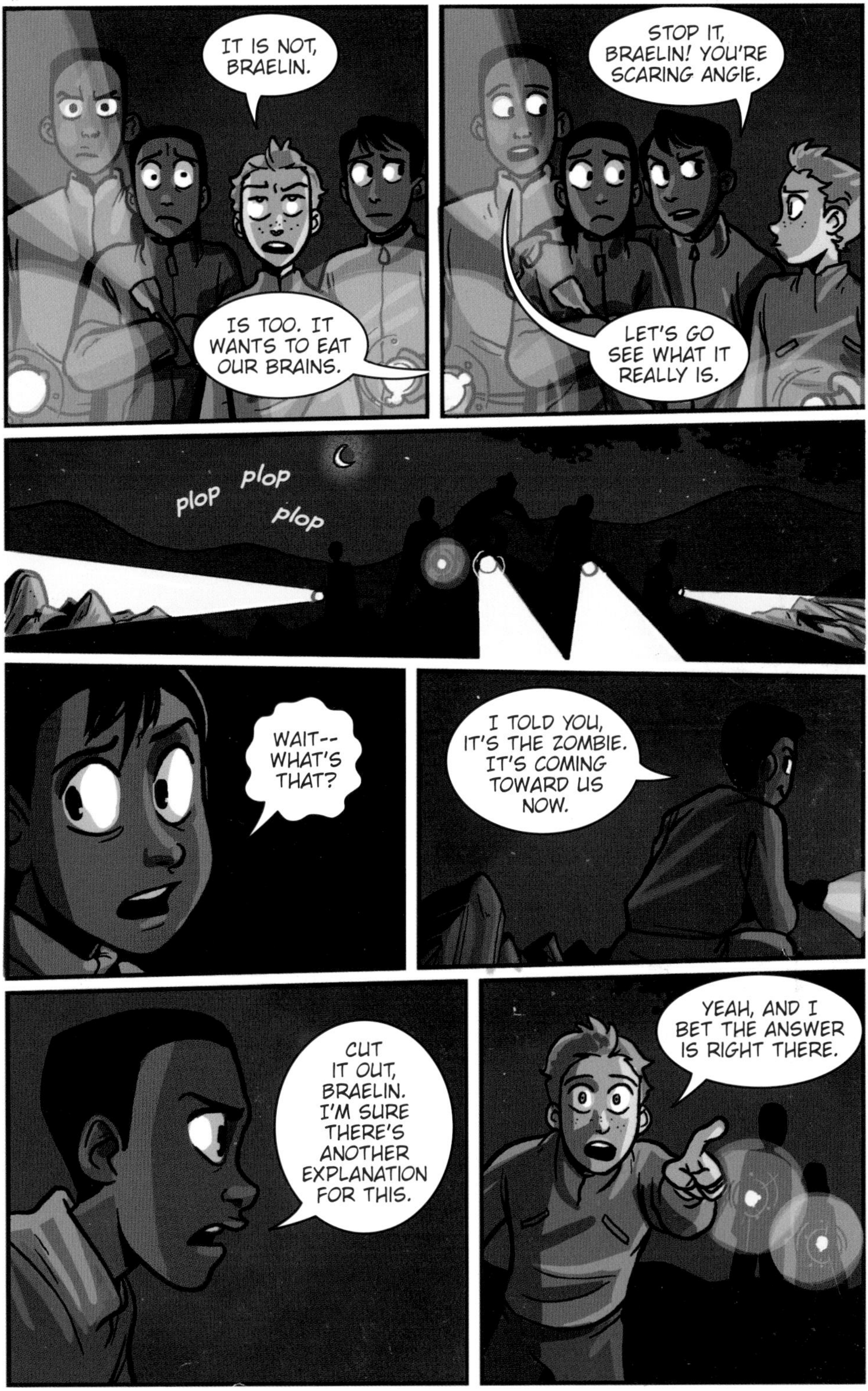
IT IS NOT, BRAELIN.
IS TOO. IT WANTS TO EAT OUR BRAINS.
STOP IT, BRAELIN! YOU'RE SCARING ANGIE.
LET'S GO SEE WHAT IT REALLY IS.
plop
plop
plop
WAIT-- WHAT'S THAT?
I TOLD YOU, IT'S THE ZOMBIE. IT'S COMING TOWARD US NOW.
CUT IT OUT, BRAELIN. I'M SURE THERE'S ANOTHER EXPLANATION FOR THIS.
YEAH, AND I BET THE ANSWER IS RIGHT THERE.

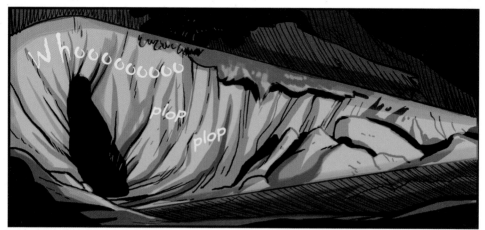

THAT'S IT? THAT'S CAMERON'S CAVERN?

I THINK SO.

I'M NOT GOING IN THERE. THAT'S WHERE THE ZOMBIE IS!

I DON'T WANT MY BRAINS TO GET EATEN!

DO YOU WANT TO STAY OUT HERE BY YOURSELF?

NO!

IT'S OKAY, ANGIE. WE'LL PROTECT YOU.

I'LL STAY RIGHT NEXT TO YOU. COME ON.

OKAY, LET'S GO.

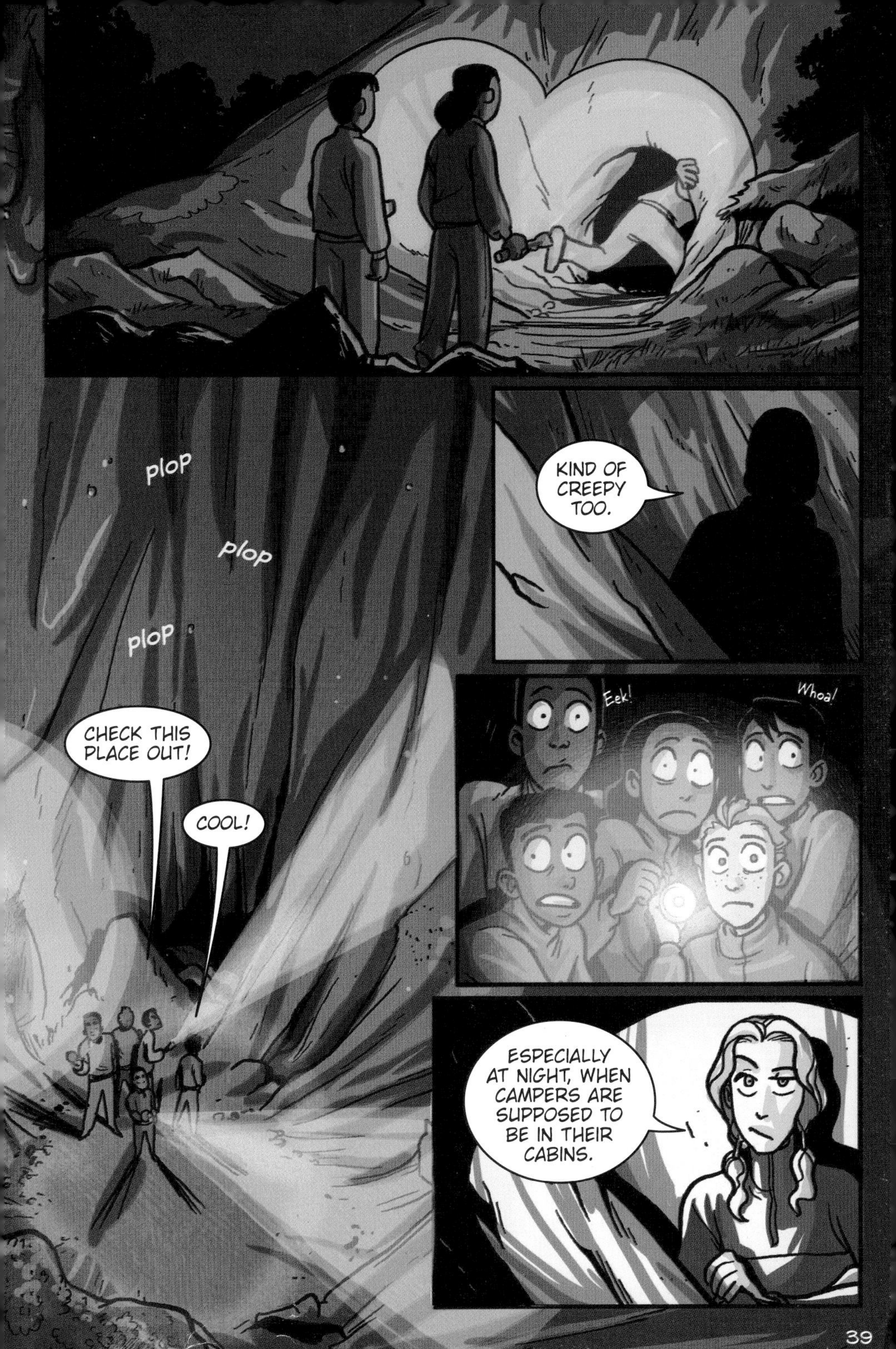
plop
plop
plop
CHECK THIS PLACE OUT!
COOL!
KIND OF CREEPY TOO.
Eek!
Whoa!
ESPECIALLY AT NIGHT, WHEN CAMPERS ARE SUPPOSED TO BE IN THEIR CABINS.

I'M REALLY SORRY...

WE JUST...

WE WERE LOOKING FOR...

I KNEW CURIOSITY WOULD GET THE BEST OF YOU. WELL, YOU'RE HERE NOW. YOU MIGHT AS WELL LOOK AROUND.

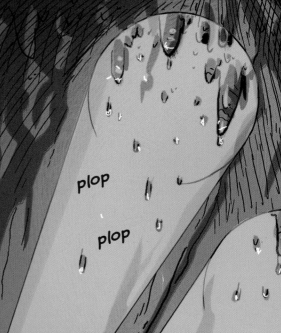

plop

plop

HEY, THAT SOUNDS LIKE THE ZOMBIE FOOTSTEPS.

IT'S JUST WATER DRIPPING OFF THE CEILING ONTO THE ROCKS BELOW.

BUT WHY IS THERE WATER UP THERE?

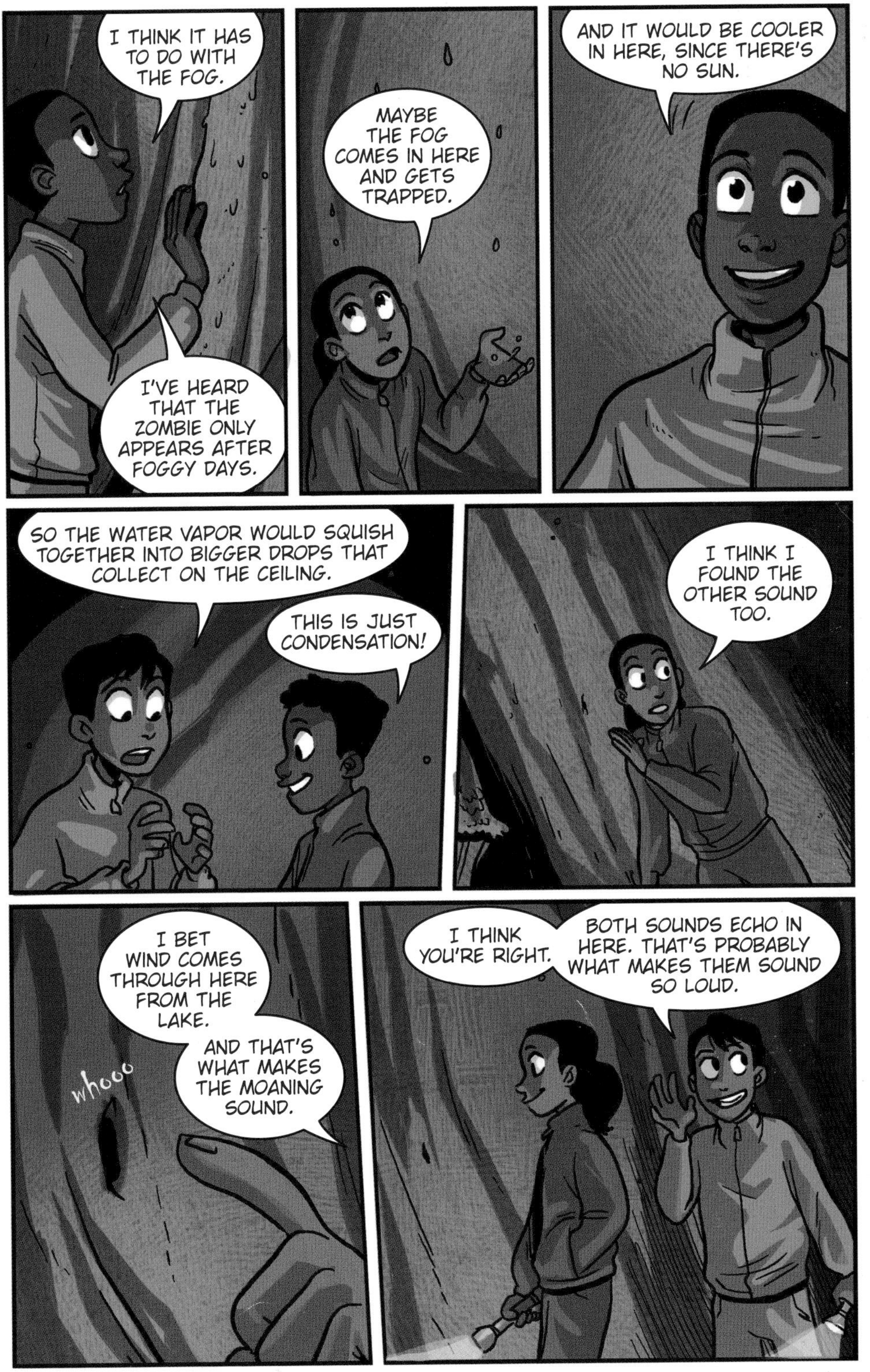
I THINK IT HAS TO DO WITH THE FOG.
I'VE HEARD THAT THE ZOMBIE ONLY APPEARS AFTER FOGGY DAYS.
MAYBE THE FOG COMES IN HERE AND GETS TRAPPED.
AND IT WOULD BE COOLER IN HERE, SINCE THERE'S NO SUN.
SO THE WATER VAPOR WOULD SQUISH TOGETHER INTO BIGGER DROPS THAT COLLECT ON THE CEILING.
THIS IS JUST CONDENSATION!
I THINK I FOUND THE OTHER SOUND TOO.
I BET WIND COMES THROUGH HERE FROM THE LAKE.
AND THAT'S WHAT MAKES THE MOANING SOUND.
whooo
I THINK YOU'RE RIGHT.
BOTH SOUNDS ECHO IN HERE. THAT'S PROBABLY WHAT MAKES THEM SOUND SO LOUD.

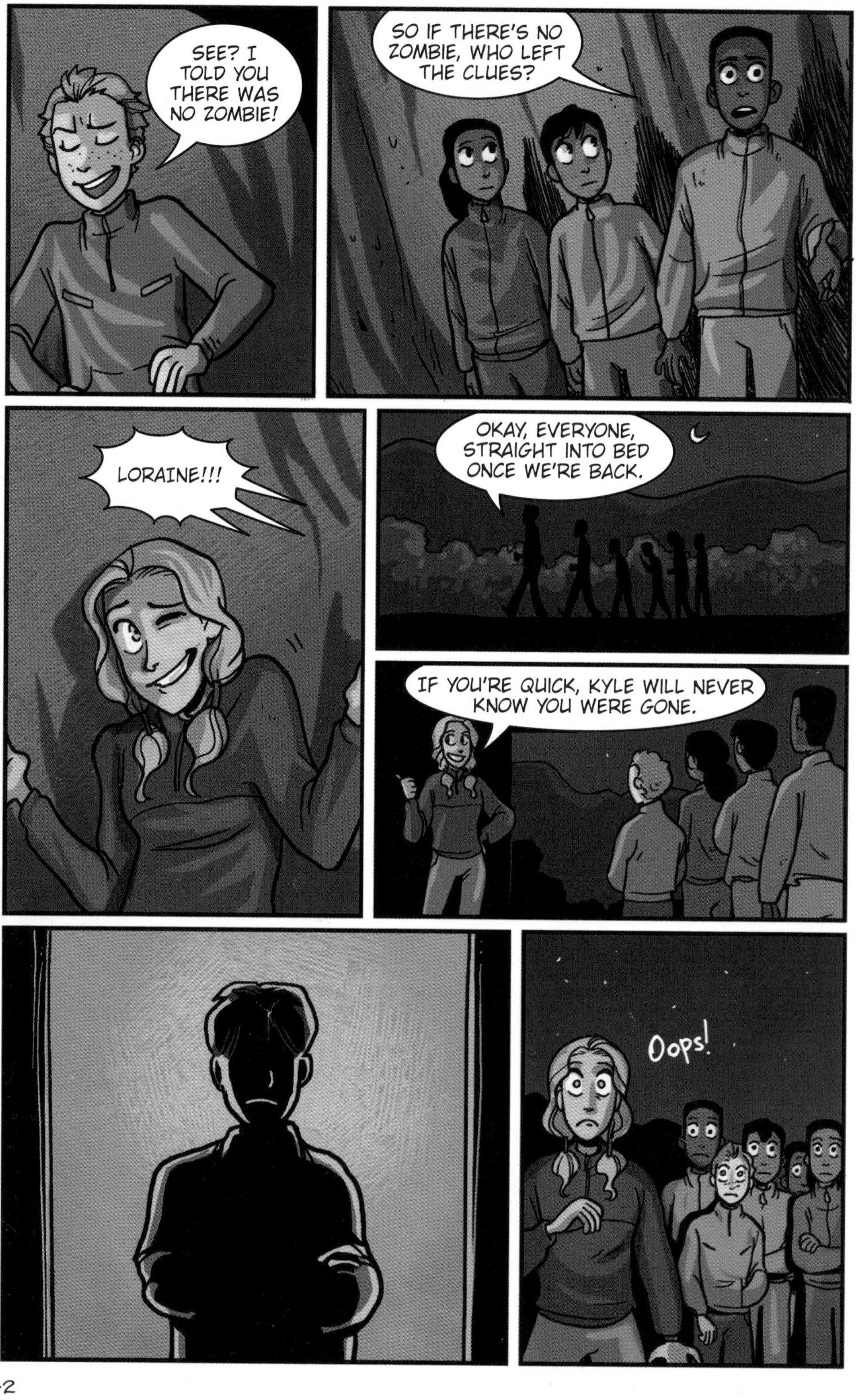
SEE? I TOLD YOU THERE WAS NO ZOMBIE!
SO IF THERE'S NO ZOMBIE, WHO LEFT THE CLUES?
LORAINE!!!
OKAY, EVERYONE, STRAIGHT INTO BED ONCE WE'RE BACK.
IF YOU'RE QUICK, KYLE WILL NEVER KNOW YOU WERE GONE.
Oops!

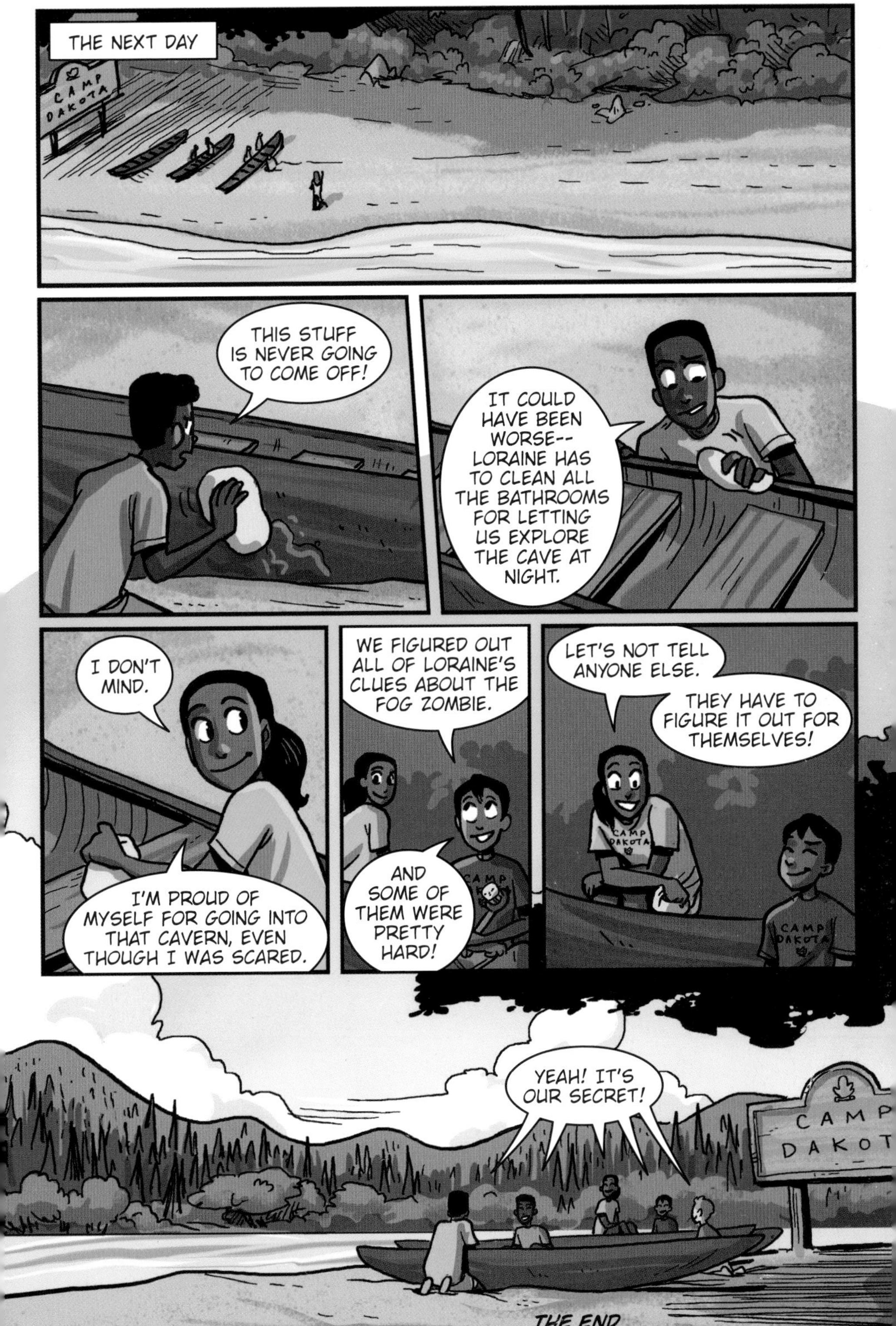
THE NEXT DAY
CAMP DAKOTA
THIS STUFF IS NEVER GOING TO COME OFF!
IT COULD HAVE BEEN WORSE-- LORAINE HAS TO CLEAN ALL THE BATHROOMS FOR LETTING US EXPLORE THE CAVE AT NIGHT.
I DON'T MIND.
I'M PROUD OF MYSELF FOR GOING INTO THAT CAVERN, EVEN THOUGH I WAS SCARED.
WE FIGURED OUT ALL OF LORAINE'S CLUES ABOUT THE FOG ZOMBIE.
AND SOME OF THEM WERE PRETTY HARD!
LET'S NOT TELL ANYONE ELSE.
THEY HAVE TO FIGURE IT OUT FOR THEMSELVES!
CAMP DAKOTA
CAMP DAKOTA
YEAH! IT'S OUR SECRET!
CAMP DAKOT
THE END

Experiments

Try these fun experiments at home or in your classroom.
Make sure you have an adult help out.

Cloud in a Jar

You will need: glass jar, hot water from a faucet, a small metal tray or bowl, ice cubes, black construction paper, tape, a match

1) Tape the black construction paper onto the back of the glass jar, so you can only see into the jar from the front.

2) Fill the glass jar about one-third full with hot water.

3) Swirl the hot water around the jar for a few seconds to warm the sides.

4) Have an adult light a match, blow it out, and drop the match into the jar.

5) Place the metal tray on top of the glass jar.

6) Pile ice cubes on top of the metal tray.

7) Watch carefully for a cloud to form inside the jar.

What happened?

The hot water evaporated into water vapor. The ice cooled the air at the top of the jar. When the water vapor came in contact with the cooler air, it condensed into water droplets on the smoke particles. All those tiny droplets make up a cloud.

Wire Stretch

You will need: copper wire; a small, heavy object, such as a bell; two chairs; string; candle; a box

Make sure you get help from an adult for this experiment.

1) Set the two chairs a few feet apart.

2) Attach the copper wire to the two chairs, pulling it taut.

3) Place the box between the two chairs.

4) Using the string, attach the small, heavy object to the middle of the wire line.

5) Adjust the string so that the object is hanging about an inch above the box.

6) Light the candle, and hold the flame near the copper wire. Move it back and forth along the wire.

7) Keep the candle away from the string and chairs. Do not touch the wire.

8) As the wire heats up, the object will sink until it rests on the box.

9) Remove the candle, and allow the wire to cool down. The object will be suspended again.

What happened?

Energy, in the form of heat, was transferred to the wire. That made the molecules in the wire move farther apart and take up more space. The wire expanded, which allowed it to sag under the weight of the object.

When the energy source was taken away, the molecules slowed down and moved closer together, contracting the wire and lifting the object again.

Mysterious Words

atom: the smallest part of matter

condensation: the process of changing from a gas to liquid

density: a measure of mass per unit of volume

element: a substance that is made entirely from one type of atom

evaporation: the process of changing from a liquid into a gas

mass: the amount of matter in something

molecule: two or more atoms joined together

particle: a single part, or piece, of matter

volume: the amount of space that matter takes up

Could YOU have solved the mystery of the fog zombie?

Good thing the kids of Camp Dakota knew a bit about matter—and got some helpful tips from the counselors. See if you caught all the facts they put to use.

- Everything is made of different kinds of atoms, or elements. The periodic table of the elements is a chart that shows the chemical symbols and several properties of each element.

- Many substances can change between a gas, liquid, or solid state. Water does this when it freezes into ice or condenses on the ceiling of a cave, for example.

- Fog is a cloud near the ground, made up of tiny water droplets in the air. Fog forms when cool temperatures cause water vapor in the air to condense into droplets that are small and light enough to float. Fog and clouds disappear when heat, such as from the sun, causes the water droplets to evaporate (change into water vapor).

- Matter particles come in different sizes and shapes. When you combine things that are different sizes, the amount of space they take up may be different from the total space they take up separately.

- Packing more particles into the same amount of space increases the density of matter.

- Gases, such as air, take up space even though they are made up of particles too small to see.

- Molecules within a substance move faster and spread out when they heat up. That makes things swell or stretch when they get hot.

THE AUTHOR

LYNDA BEAUREGARD wrote her first story when she was seven years old and hasn't stopped writing since. She also likes teaching kids how to swim, designing websites, directing race cars out onto the track, and throwing bouncy balls for her cat, Becca. She lives near Detroit, Michigan, with her two lovely daughters, who are doing their best to turn her hair gray.

THE ARTISTS

DER-SHING HELMER graduated from University of California–Berkeley, where she played with snakes and lizards all summer long. When she is not teaching biology to high school students, she is making art and comics for everyone to enjoy. Her best friends are her two pet geckos (Smeg and Jerry), her king snake (Clarice), and the chinchilla that lives next door.

GUILLERMO MOGORRÓN started drawing before he could walk or talk. When he is not drawing monsters or spaceships piloted by monkeys, he loves to fight with his cat and walk his dog. He also enjoys meeting friends and reading comics. He lives near Madrid, Spain.

GERMAN TORRES has always loved to draw. He also likes to drive his van to the mountains and enjoy a little fresh air with his girlfriend and dogs. But what he really loves is traveling. He lives in a town near Barcelona, Spain, away from the noise of the city.